Attacks
?

5

Dachima Inaka

Illustration by **Iida Pochi.**

"Adventuring with my son brings me such joy!"

For the inaugural issue of *Maman*, the mom magazine covering all the hottest topics in the game world, we've compiled a special feature on Mamako Oosuki. So many of you asked to get to know her better that we conducted an impromptu interview with Mamako herself!

Mamako "Good afternoon…or is it evening? I'm Mamako Oosuki. Nice to meet you!"

Let's all resist the urge to rest our heads on her lap and see what she has to say.

The secret to beauty is adventuring with your children!

You must get this a lot, but you really are quite beautiful.

Mamako "Oh, my. You know how to flatter a woman!"

It's not flattery, just my genuine, honest opinion. You're the mother of a high-school boy—what's the secret to maintaining your youthful beauty?

Mamako "I don't think I do anything special… Oh, I know. I'm adventuring with my son! Perhaps that's why."

I doubt adventuring has any effect on one's beauty…

Mamako "Being with my son, Ma-kun, going to all sorts of places, experiencing all kinds of things, talking about this and that… It brings me such joy! Hee-hee!"

So Masato's presence revitalizes you.

Mamako "And not just Ma-kun! Wise and Medhi and Porta always keep me going strong. I have them all to thank!"

Adventuring in the game world with your beloved son and wonderful companions. That time together makes you shine like no other.

Leave housework and battles to Mommy!

You handle all the housework and serve as the party's main powerhouse in battle. Sounds like every day is as busy as it is enjoyable.

Mamako "Sometimes it's certainly a lot of work, but it's very fulfilling."

You're indomitable! No enemies stand a chance against you. But some think you work a bit too hard.

Mamako "That's true… Ma-kun often yells at me for overdoing it. But…while we're together like this, I want to do everything I can…"

You know he'll leave the nest someday, so you want to mother him while you still can. All parents feel that way.

Mamako "Leave the nest… Someday Ma-kun will leave me… Oh, I feel faint…"

Whoaaa?! Mamakooo?!

(The interviewer used restorative medicine.)

(Mamako regained consciousness!)

Entering the World Matriarchal Arts Tournament!

A-anyway, Mamako needs to get her shopping done, so time for one final question. Will you be entering the World Matriarchal Arts Tournament?

Mamako "Yes, I'm planning to."

What are you hoping to achieve there?

Mamako "I'll do whatever I can to make some precious memories with my son and obtain a wonderful prize."

She already has victory in her sights?! We can't miss this!

MAMAN

SPECIAL REPORT

MAMAKO OOSUKI
INTERVIEW

CHILD MAMAKO

For...reasons, Mamako has turned into a child. She looks to be about five years old, but inside she's the same as ever, and her son still has to treat her as his mom—meaning more problems for him.

"I'm still Mommy, even if I'm tiny! I'm gonna spoil you sooo much!"

ANIMAL MAMAKO

Somehow she has animal ears now. And two tails, naturally. With her heightened animal instincts, Mamako's new perceptive powers pose further problems for her son.

"Am I a doggie? Or maybe a kitty? But I'm still Mommy, bow-meow!"

"Come follow Devil Mommy on an excursion!"

DEVIL MAMAKO

Possessed by a peculiar ghost, Mamako has transformed into a devil. This race feeds off human energy, but all she requires is her son's, so he's the only one who has a problem with it.

"Spend eternity with Mommy in the Mother Forest."

ELF MAMAKO

Mamako's elf form after drinking the elf potion. The blonde hair and pointy ears are quite striking. She can now hear the voices of plants and trees, but she can hear her son's voice better than anything, which causes him problems.

HAHAKO

A mysterious mother who enters the World Matriarchal Arts Tournament opposite Mamako, to whom she bears a striking resemblance. Hahako sees Mamako as her enemy, and insists that Masato is actually her son, but…

"If I defeat you, then I'll be the strongest, and I'll be Masato's mother."

CONTENTS

Dachima Inaka

DO YOU
LOVE YOUR
MOM
and Her Two-Hit
Multi-Target
Attacks
?

VOLUME 5

DACHIMA INAKA

Illustration by IIDA POCHI.

YEN
ON

New York

Do You Love Your Mom and Her Two-Hit Multi-Target Attacks?, Vol. 5

▶ Dachima Inaka

▶ Translation by Andrew Cunningham

▶ Cover art by Iida Pochi.

TSUJO KOGEKI GA ZENTAI KOGEKI DE 2KAI KOGEKI NO OKASAN WA SUKI DESUKA? Vol. 5
©Dachima Inaka, Iida Pochi. 2018
First published in Japan in 2018 by KADOKAWA CORPORATION, Tokyo.
English translation rights arranged with KADOKAWA CORPORATION, Tokyo,
through TUTTLE-MORI AGENCY, INC., Tokyo.

English translation © 2020 by Yen Press, LLC

First Yen On Edition: March 2020

Yen On is an imprint of Yen Press, LLC.
The Yen On name and logo are trademarks of Yen Press, LLC.

The publisher is not responsible for websites (or their content) that are not owned by the publisher.

▶ Yen On
  150 West 30th Street, 19th Floor
  New York, NY 10001

▶ Visit us at yenpress.com
  facebook.com/yenpress
  twitter.com/yenpress
  yenpress.tumblr.com
  instagram.com/yenpress

Library of Congress Cataloging-in-Publication Data
Names: Inaka, Dachima, author. | Pochi., Iida, illustrator. |
    Cunningham, Andrew, 1979– translator.
Title: Do you love your mom and her two-hit multi-target attacks? /
    Dachima Inaka ; illustration by Iida Pochi. ; translation by
    Andrew Cunningham.
Other titles: Tsujo kogeki ga zentai kogeki de 2kai kogeki no
    okasan wa suki desuka?. English
Description: First Yen On edition. | New York : Yen On, 2018–
Identifiers: LCCN 2018030739 | ISBN 9781975328009 (v. 1 : pbk.) |
    ISBN 9781975328375 (v. 2 : pbk.) | ISBN 9781975328399 (v. 3 : pbk.) |
    ISBN 9781975328412 (v. 4 : pbk.) | ISBN 9781975359423 (v. 5 : pbk.)
Subjects: LCSH: Virtual reality—Fiction.
Classification: LCC PL871.5.N35 T7813 2018 | DDC 895.63/6—dc23
LC record available at https://lccn.loc.gov/2018030739

ISBNs: 978-1-9753-5942-3 (paperback)
       978-1-9753-0949-7 (ebook)

10 9 8 7 6 5 4 3 2 1

LSC-C

Printed in the United States of America

Prologue   An Application from a Certain Mother

Name of participant:
My name is Mamako Oosuki.
Occupation:
I'm a Normal Hero's Mother. (In the real world, I'm a housewife.)
Number of children:
I have one.
Children's names:
His name is Ma-kun (Masato).
Special skills:
Nothing to brag about, but I'm good at all kinds of housework.
Equipment:
The Holy Sword of Mother Earth, Terra di Madre (the red one).
The Holy Sword of Mother Ocean, Altura (the blue one).
For armor, I have my favorite dress and some defensive pieces.
Acquired skills and spells:
I can't use magic, but I think I've learned most skills a mother should.
Availability for matches:
I have laundry in the mornings, so if the assembly and match start times are too early, I may not be able to make it.
In the afternoons, I need to take the laundry off the line and go shopping for dinner, so it would be a big help if we could wrap things up by three.
Please list your aspirations for this tournament:
Thank you so much for inviting me!
I'm not the most competitive person, but the prize is so wonderful, and I think Ma-kun would be simply delighted, so I'm going to do my best!

*   *   *

She finished filling out the application.

"Say, Ma-kun, what do you think? Let me know if anything sounds weird."

Mamako came over to him, pressing the pop-up window screen in his face. Pressing up against him. The screen, too. All of it right in his face. Too close for comfort.

One second he was lounging around their room in the inn, and the next, this.

Forced to check the contents of the window with it pressed too close to comfortably see, Masato tried to read it over...but immediately frowned and let out a long sigh.

"Yeah...there are so many things wrong here."

"Like what?"

"First, you're being way too polite. You don't need to use full sentences for your name or occupation! What if they end up registering you with that stuff included?"

"Oh, good point... Then my name would be Ms. My name is Mamako Oosuki. Hee-hee!"

"Don't even joke about that... And, like, for the child's name..."

What is the name of Ms. My name is Mamako Oosuki's child?

His name is Ma-kun (Masato).

"Why is my actual name in parenthesis?! Don't put my nickname in an application!"

"Oh, gosh! How careless of me! Mommy always calls you Ma-kun, so that's just the first thing I think of."

"Please at least correct that part! I'm begging you! Also..."

The next part was critical.

Masato quickly read over the form again and voiced the most pressing question.

"Uh, Mom... What is this application for? It says *tournament* here, but..."

"Well..." Mamako hesitated, and then an idea hit her. "Actually, I think it's best to keep this secret until the day of."

"Hang on... What's the point of that?"

"This way, it can be a special surprise from Mommy to you! With love! Hee-hee."

"No, no, please fill me in now. I need advance warning for these things… Telling me it's a surprise just makes me anxious. The anxiety is already killing me."

Coming from the super-OP Mamako, his actual mother, a surprise always came with a cost.

Something was brewing… Something he would never expect but would absolutely place an enormous burden on his shoulders.

This was bad news.

"Hee-hee-hee! Mommy's so excited!"

"You're giving me an ulcer!"

There were few things more terrifying to Masato than his mother's unexplained excitement.

And with that gentle smile and look of anguished horror, another delightful family adventure began.

Chapter 1 Mom's the Star of the Show! The Hero Son Does Odd Jobs! This Is How It Always Is, and It Sucks.

All heroes grow stronger by conquering whatever harsh trials their adventures have in store for them.

Each had a firm grasp on their role.

"...All right. Formation: single row. Everyone, line up!"

With confidence befitting a leader, the hero, Masato, barked orders, and his companions quickly obeyed.

"Ha-ha! This is my moment! Time to taste the power of the ultimate Sage!"

Next to him, in a crimson sorcerer's jacket, eyes burning with the red light of battle, was the party Sage, Wise.

Next to her was the Cleric, Medhi, clad in the purest white.

"Every party needs a healer. I provide that service and am equally an asset in combat. With me along, victory is assured!"

Beside her was a twelve-year-old Traveling Merchant named Porta, keeping a tight grip on her trademark shoulder bag.

"I'll help, too! I can be useful!"

With the girls lined up behind Masato, they were ready for anything.

Masato glanced down the row, encouraged by their presence.

"Right!" he said. "Okay, everyone... Places! Ready! Set!"

The four knelt, like a race was about to start. Ready to dash forward and reach the battle zone as fast as possible.

All eyes locked onto the final member of their party.

A pleasant breeze blew across the sun-drenched field, and she was humming, her generous bosom swaying as she traipsed along.

Masato's mother, Mamako.

"It's such a lovely day! I'm so glad I packed lunches for us. Let's get this quest completed and have a picnic! Hee-hee!"

But a pack of monsters appeared in the direction she was walking!

Centipedes and moles! Vicious insects and beasts alike!

"Oh my! Could these be the monsters they told us about?"

Their current quest objective was to exterminate these monsters. Now, to combat!

However:

"M-Masato! Monsters in front of Mama!"

"Yeah, I know... But wait a sec. Remain on standby."

They held their formation, crouched and at the ready, assessing the situation, waiting for the perfect moment.

Mamako engaged the monsters.

"Then Mommy's gonna defeat them! Hyah!"

Mamako attacked, swinging the two Holy Swords in her hands. A two-hit multi-target attack that divvied up the damage between all foes!

The Holy Sword of Earth, Terra di Madre! Its power caused massive rock spikes to shoot out of the ground!

The Holy Sword of the Ocean, Altura! Its power turned water into bullets, peppering their foes!

The monsters were sliced and diced and impaled and slain!

Mamako defeated the monsters! Combat complete!

The very next moment:

"Okay! Now!"

"Let's go! Chaaaaaarge!"

"Now's our chance to prove our strength!"

"R-right! I'm coming, too!"

The moment combat was over, the rest of the party broke into a run and headed for where the monsters had fallen.

The defeated monsters turned to dust, leaving behind dice-shaped materials known as gems, which could be exchanged for money. "I'll gather all the gems I can!" cried Porta. "Go for it!" cheered Masato. Gem gathering was Porta's key duty. They left that to her.

But it wasn't only gems that the monsters left behind.

On rare occasions, some monsters would leave items—the proverbial drop item.

This was their fight.

"Wise! Medhi! You know the rules! If they drop an item..."

"If we catch it before it hits the ground, we win!"

"If they hit the ground, we lose!"

"That's right! That's the rule! This is our true battle! We racked our brains in desperation and finally found something we can dooooo!"

Mamako's mega-firepower was all ordinary combat required.

But even so, the rest of the party wanted to do *something*.

They spied a paperlike drop item fluttering in the air as it fell!

"Rahhhhhhh! Sliding caaaatch!!" yelled Masato.

"Oh, crap! The one over there's about to hit the ground! Nooooooo!" Wise hollered.

"Wise!" shouted Medhi. "Time to chain cast! Use the wind to lift it into the air and prevent it from falling!"

"Oh my! Everyone's so fired up! Hee-hee!"

The party mother watched them with a pleasant smile.

The children were soon covered in grass stains, mud, and tears.

A battle for the safety of the realm and a battle for the safety of their self-worth.

With both battles complete, the party gathered around their loot.

"We really went into that battle with guns blazing, if you ignore how pathetic it all was... But what are these things?" Masato wondered.

He had obtained...several pieces of paper.

All identical. All suspiciously flyer-like.

WORLD MATRIARCHAL ARTS TOURNAMENT! COMING SOON!

That tournament name seemed suspiciously familiar. Below the banner was an illustration of a mother holding a frying pan lid.

It also claimed that applications were flooding in, said an official pamphlet would be provided to anyone who visited the venue, and described how to access the town where this was being held.

At the very bottom of the flyer were a number of coupons that could be used at town shops during the tournament. Discounts as high as five percent. Not especially meaningful.

But anyway, these were their drop items.

"Wise, Medhi, what'd you get?" asked Masato.

"The same flyers you got," answered Wise.

"Me too," replied Medhi. "It seems like all drops from that group of monsters were set to these flyers."

"Maybe it's a special flyer! I'll check it out!"

"No, no point, Porta," said Masato. "Even if you appraise them... they're just junk."

Masato balled them up and was about to toss them.

"W-wait, Ma-kun!" Mamako said, stopping him. "You can't just throw them away!"

"Oh, right, right, no littering... But they're still junk, so we're getting rid of them."

"D-don't say that! See? There are discount coupons!"

"I know you love that sort of thing, but...I just don't care..."

"And—and look! There's a tournament! Doesn't that sound fun? Ma-kun, you like tournaments! I thought you'd be excited about that!"

"Hmm... I mean, the name of the tournament is certainly dicey, so it definitely caught my attention in that regard, but...problem is..."

The World Matriarchal *Arts Tournament*.

"Can I even enter this?"

"I'm afraid you can't, Ma-kun. Only mothers can enter."

"Huh. So you're saying this tournament is only for moms and I can't participate... Hmm..."

"But look! If you join the audience, you can see all the moms doing their very best! Witness moms in the heat of battle and cheer them on!"

"That's...not the worst thing, I guess..."

"So then—!"

"Oh, but...I swore a vow to never get baited by another flyer again. I've learned the hard way not to take Shiraaase's bait, and this could be another trap set by the Four Heavenly Kings..."

"Don't worry! This time it's definitely an event planned by the admins. It's just moms fighting; nothing bad will happen to you!"

"Interesting. So since this is an official event, we can just relax and watch it happen?"

"That's right! All you have to do is watch the matches! So...!"

That was what made him suspicious.

"Mom, just one question…"

"Yes? What?"

"This flyer doesn't say anything about who can join the tournament or about it being an official game event… So…what's your source on that?"

"S-sauce…? If you've got a favorite sauce, I'm happy to use that in the future…"

"No, not condiments! Source! Where'd you get your information?"

"W-well… Um… It's sort of hard to explain…"

"Ugh, look, it's time to come clean. Mom, you already knew about this tournament, and for some reason, you're trying to convince us to go there."

"That's… Well… Not exactly wrong…"

"Okay, let's start with you telling us why," Masato said, getting extremely irritated. "If we don't know that, we're not going anywhere. So come on! Spit it out!"

At this point, the girls stepped in to defend Mamako.

"Hey! Masato! Knock it off!" yelled Wise. "I thought you'd grown out of that!"

"I've been told you often yelled at Mamako for not explaining things when you first got sent to this world," said Medhi.

"Masato! Please! Calm down a little!" pleaded Porta.

"Y-yeah, yeah, okay. I haven't forgotten that; don't worry. I'm not trying to make the same mistakes again. The consequences aren't worth it."

Children were better off never seeing their parents look that sad.

Masato's aggressive questioning had certainly left Mamako flustered, but she had not yet grown crestfallen. He hadn't crossed that line yet. He could still dial it back.

Masato took a deep breath, willing himself to be calm, to find his gentle side. And then he asked once more.

"Um… Mom, do you mind?"

"N-no, go ahead."

"Clearly, you'd like us to go to this tournament. As the audience."

"Yes. That's right."

"And there's a reason for that."

"There is. But… Well, I was given some advice, you see. That it would be best to reveal that reason on the day of the tournament. That it would be a nice surprise for you all."

"And there's only one person we know prone to unnecessary 'advice' like that…"

Setting aside the identity of the culprit who'd infooormed Mamako…

This was a tournament for moms. And Mamako wanted them to attend.

And the specific reasons would be revealed the day of the tournament.

These facts were enough for him to guess the rest. So he went right for the heart of it.

"Mom…are you thinking about joining this World Matriarchal Arts Tournament?"

He was definitely not big on that idea.

But Mamako went red like an embarrassed schoolgirl.

"Gosh, Ma-kun! You can't just say that out loud! Eek!"

She fidgeted for a moment and then nodded. "Mamako, you're so cuuuute!" "A blushing maiden." "Adorable!" It was a big hit with the girls anyway.

But for a son hit with the full force of his mother's blushing maiden routine?

"…Guh……"

He collapsed, coughing up blood. His mother's cuteness was too much for him to bear.

With their extermination quest completed, the party returned to the nearby inn town so they could report their achievement to the Adventurers Guild. Any monsters they encountered along the way were dispatched by Mamako with a "Hyah!" and posed no threat at all.

Masato was feeling dizzy—and not just from loss of blood.

"Entering a tournament? Mom, what are you thinking…? That's so not your thing…"

"True, but I've got my eye on the grand prize!"

"Wow, Mamako, it's not every day you get so fired up about something like that," marveled Wise.

"What exactly is the prize?" asked Medhi.

"I want to know! Please tell us!" said Porta.

"Hee-hee… Well…here!"

Ta-daa! Mamako pulled out a piece of paper from between her breasts. "Why was it in there?!" "Well, this dress doesn't have any pockets…" She'd been keeping it close to her chest, literally.

Unlike the tournament flyers they'd found, this piece of paper had a grand prize listed: a Mother-Child Album. It looked like any other photo album.

But this was no ordinary album. According to the description, it had a function that would automatically preserve memorable scenes the parent and child experienced together within this game.

Masato didn't see that as anything worth celebrating.

"Auto-capturing our adventures? I can see why you'd like that…but I'm terrified it'll be preserving all the traumatic memories, too…"

Scenes of Mamako leaving Masato in her dust as she took care of everything or scenes of her wearing all sorts of horrifying costumes… Scenes that were bad enough witnessing in person preserved in vivid detail…

"Ugh… That's the last thing I need…"

"Maybe for you it is," said Wise, "but for Mamako, every moment with you is a precious treasure."

"Exactly!" agreed Mamako. "Honestly, I wanted to bring a camera and take lots of pictures of you for me to cherish…but I forgot…"

"So this prize is exactly the thing she most wants," said Medhi.

"It's a very rare item! I think we should get it!" said Porta.

"A rare item, huh…? I do like the sound of that… But still…"

He would really rather not get this one.

Maybe he could talk her out of entering. He considered trying…

…but then he looked at her.

"What could be more wonderful than a book full of memories with Ma-kun? Hee-hee!"

She just looked so happy. Happier than he'd ever seen her.

Seeing her this happy even made Masato start to smile.

And of course, that changed his mind.

I shouldn't just give up this easily…

He shouldn't. He definitely shouldn't.

This was definitely something he should stick to his guns on.

But another part of him felt like forcing his opinions on everyone was really childish.

My feelings versus Mom's feelings... Which is more important? ...This is so hard...

He choked back the protest welling up within, electing to put off his qualms for another day.

And he realized they'd already reached town.

They walked down a bustling road lined with shops selling items and provisions, heading for the Adventurers Guild.

It was a plain building, like a government office. They went to the reception desk, and the girl behind it came over, smiling at them.

"Oh, Mamako Oosuki and children. Well done."

"Let's try that again. This time, say 'The hero and his party.'"

"Geez, Masato. You pick the weirdest things to get all worked up over," scolded Wise.

"Hello!" greeted Mamako. "We're here to report the quest completion."

While Masato spluttered, Mamako and the guild lady completed the paperwork. Mamako drew up the extermination report, had the guild lady verify it, and received the reward.

Mamako had known little about games in general and had been perplexed by many of the mechanics, but she was really starting to get a handle on this type of thing. Like a proper leader.

Medhi and Porta seemed quite impressed.

"It didn't take long for Mamako to become a proper adventurer!" admired Wise.

"She's a really reliable adventurer mom!" agreed Porta.

"And where does that leave me? *Sigh...* Guess I'm getting used to it."

Their reward accepted, they were done here. Masato tucked his tail between his legs, and they left the guild...

Nope. Before they did, he had a question for the guild lady.

"Oh, that's right! Mind if I ask you something? When we defeated the monsters, they dropped these flyers for something called the World Matriarchal Arts Tournament..."

"If you pass those out to people in town, you can receive a reward," replied the guild lady. "The more you pass out, the higher the payout! You should definitely try it."

"You're making adventurers pass out flyers for you? I mean, maybe it's a decent way to make a little pocket money..."

"Ah, speaking of the World Matriarchal Arts Tournament, we have packages for Mamako."

The guild lady started rummaging beneath the counter.

She pulled out a bundle of envelopes, some leather-bound books, the kind of scrolls ninja arts are written on, a giant leaf, an object that looked suspiciously like a memory stick—quite a lot of things all lined up in front of Mamako.

"Oh my, all of these? Whatever for?"

"It seems the other tournament participants have sent you challenges."

"Huh? Challenges? To Mom? ...Whoa, there's all this stuff written on them."

He looked around—every one of them said *Challenge* on it. Even the giant leaf had *I look forward to facing you!* written clearly on the back.

"Why would anyone challenge Mom? And so many people...in so many formats..."

"Mothers from many different races are hoping to face off against Mamako."

"Different races... True, we did meet an elf before, but are there others?"

"Of course! Quite a few."

"I had no idea... And people...mothers...from these races...want to fight my mom?"

"There are many people who admire her. Mamako was on the cover of the inaugural issue of *Maman* magazine, and the special feature on the World Matriarchal Arts Tournament mentioned her as a strong candidate to take the top prize. It's only natural she'd attract a lot of attention."

"What? Uh... What the heck is *Maman*...?"

"A monthly magazine for mothers. You haven't heard of it?"

It was sold all over the world and read avidly by mothers everywhere. "Mommy got interviewed by them!" "And you're just mentioning this now?!" Without her son's knowledge, his mother's fame continued to rise.

"So this tournament is pretty famous...?" asked Masato.

"I would imagine all mothers and those who admire them know about it. I, too, wish to become a mother someday, so I have been paying close attention to this... Mm? Huh?"

The guild lady suddenly tilted her head, staring at Mamako.

"Mamako, have you already passed the prelims?"

"Huh? The prelims?" Mamako looked confused.

Just then, there was a loud thud that shook the entire guild building. The noise came from right outside.

"Wh-what the heck? Did something crash-land in the street?" Masato wondered aloud. "We'd better check it out!"

The party ran out the door to find a small crater in front of the Adventurers Guild...

...and a coffin standing upright in the center of it.

"Ma-kun, Mommy's noticed that when we find coffins, it's always—"

"Yeah. *Her.* She sure picked a flashy way to die this time..."

"Think she used a transport spell but died from the impact of the landing?" Wise hypothesized. "Not like that's usually fatal, but..."

"Anyway, we'd better bring her back and hear what she has to say," commented Medhi.

"Okay! Let's get infooormed!" said Porta.

Resurrection spells were a Cleric's specialty, so Medhi took care of it. "Now, then... Conforto Staff!" "Just cast the spell!" Medhi was being stingy with her MP, so she used a wand that randomly cast spells she'd learned.

It took about twenty attempts, but at last, a resurrection spell activated.

The coffin turned to mist, and a woman dressed as a nun appeared, her expression placid.

"Hello, Shiraaase. Yet another magnificent death you managed there," commented Masato.

"Your words honor me... Yes, I am Shiraaase. Unable to fight at all, I can infooorm you that this mysterious nun has racked up the highest death count in the— Ah, but there is no time to waste on introductions. The situation is urgent."

Shiraaase looked around, catching each party member's eye in turn. Then she raised a hand aloft.

"I'm afraid I must engage an admin's systemic power and forcibly transport all of you."

"Huh? Transport us…? Where?!"

Masato's party members were instantly transported elsewhere, not by any magic spell but by using the technology granted to those who ran the game.

Everyone opened their eyes to unfamiliar surroundings.

"Where the…?"

They were on a huge road—easily fifty yards across. It seemed to be the entrance to a town.

Looking around, they saw crowds of people of all different races: ordinary humans; pointy-eared blond elves; beastkin with animal ears and tails; and vampires resting in the shadows, presumably tired from too much sun.

Up above, they saw divine angels and spirits—and devils in disconcertingly sexy outfits flying around. Then a massive shadow briefly blotted out the sun—a flock of dragons and wyvern.

A procession of butterfly-winged fairies on a guided tour wafted past a pair of flirting giants, each over fifteen feet tall.

Basically, there was a lot going on.

Wise was puzzled. "Um, what the hell…?"

"It's like a fantasy-world character compendium!" said Medhi.

"Oooh! There are even robotic people here! Androids!" cried Porta.

"Whoa, you're right!" said Masato. "They've got jet packs! …Wait, are androids even considered fantasy? Not that I would know, but…"

Surprised and impressed, the party gawked at the races around them.

But Shiraaase urged them forward.

"This is the town where the World Matriarchal Arts Tournament is held. It's called Meema. People of all races are gathering from around the world for tomorrow's tournament. Unless using transformation spells, anyone of a race other than human is one hundred percent pure NPC. That is all."

"NPCs have purity levels?" asked Masato. "Actually, I think you've oversimplified things! Can you please tell us more about the different races? I'm really curious!"

"I'll give you a pamphlet later. You can read about the races there. First, the prelims. Come, Mamako."

"O-oh, right," said Mamako. "The prelims were today!"

"Yes. And we have very little time before they stop accepting entries. I completely forgot to tell you the deadline—I'm so sorry. But we really must hurry."

"Oh, hey!"

Shiraaase pulled Mamako quickly along.

They were headed toward a large building decorated with pots and frying pans, brooms and dustpans, hangers and clothing lines— monuments to housework. A sign with WORLD MATRIARCHAL ARTS TOURNAMENT in bold lettering was hung over the door.

At the entrance was a reception counter for participants, where a staff member was yelling "Five minutes remaining! If anyone else wants to enter, speak up now!" They really were cutting it close.

"Now, Mamako, if you would please take care of the paperwork."

"Okay! Then… Oh, but first… Ma-kun, a moment?"

"Wh-what?"

Mamako stood in front of him, her hands clasped together.

"Ma-kun, can Mommy please enter the tournament?"

"Uh… Why are you asking now?"

"Well, I know how you feel about it. Mommy applied to be in this without asking you. And I think maybe that was a mistake."

"You're always doing stuff like that, though… You never listen to me…"

"Yes. I know. I just get so happy and excited about being with you that I overdo it sometimes… So I've been thinking for a while now that I've got to try to be better…"

"You are?! Since when have you been so self-aware?!"

"So this time, I want to get your honest opinion. Ma-kun, will you tell me how you feel?"

She sounded like a timid girl who'd worked up the nerve to ask out a boy. Except this was his mom. "Gah, I can barely look her in the eye…" He was definitely getting a headache.

But this was a serious question. She was really asking.

Frankly, I'd rather she didn't enter...

At the same time, he didn't think it was right to force those feelings on her. He was trying to grow out of that sort of childishness.

But he also felt like it was a bad idea to leave things unsaid and hide how he felt.

Then what should he do? How could he make up his mind? ...Right. She was his mom.

"...Mom, since you're my mom, I'm gonna go ahead and put this out there. You ready?"

"Yes, okay. I'll accept whatever you have to say, Ma-kun. After all, I'm your mom."

Mamako smiled. Just the sight of that smile made him relax despite himself. It was the same gentle smile she always had for him. All his fretting and worrying suddenly felt silly.

Masato looked his mother directly in the eye.

"I'm not super-happy about the idea of you being in this tournament."

"I see... Then..."

"But if you want to do it, I think you should."

"...Huh?"

She looked so surprised, he immediately felt sheepish.

But he wasn't done talking. He wanted to get this all out.

"I just think...the two of us are, like, adventuring together...and I keep wanting this to be my adventure, but it's also your adventure... So this time, you should do what you want. If you want to enter the tournament, then enter it."

"...You're really sure?"

"I said I was! Your son approves! Go ahead! Even I, uh..."

Want to make you happy sometimes...proactively...

However, saying that aloud was a bit much. He swallowed the words.

"S-so, uh... Make sure you win this thing! I'll be rooting for you!"

"Oh?! You will?! You'll be rooting for Mommy?!"

"Why is that such a huge surprise? I don't think it's unusual for kids to root for their parents! I mean, I dunno how enthusiastically I'm going be cheering for you or anything, but..."

He could feel his face turning red already, and he trailed off into mumbles.

"Thank you, Ma-kun!" She started glowing fiercely.

"Ack, too brigh—MMPH?!"

Mamako threw her arms around Masato, her entire body shining brightly with A Mother's Light—a skill activated by great happiness. Masato's face was buried in blinding light, voluminous assets, luxurious softness, and his mother's sweet scent.

"Bwa?! H-hey, Mom! Too bright! Can't breathe! Calm down!"

"How can I? I've never been this happy!" *Squeeze!*

"I get that, but there's a time and a place! Everyone's staring!"

After a desperate struggle, he'd managed to get his head free and found all the girls smirking at them...

No, that wasn't true. Porta was just delighted, like she always was. Wise and Medhi both were smiling as usual, too.

"Huh? You guys aren't gonna make fun of me?"

"Why would we?" replied Wise. "We're all impressed by how much you've grown up. Like, actually putting Mamako ahead of yourself? That's a good thing!"

"Instead of just trampling your own emotions, you communicated them properly and then found the right solution on top of that," added Medhi. "That's the same thing you taught me to do, you know."

"You're really powering up as a hero son, Masato! Amazing!" cheered Porta.

"Uh... You're all...actually praising me..."

"Okay, guys, since Masato wants to cheer Mamako on, let's come up with some cheer squad stuff for him! And make it real oedipal—I mean, ostentatious!"

"You'll definitely need a fan. It should say *Mamako LOVE* on it. Or maybe *Mommy LOVE*. A *happi* coat and a headband would really complete the look."

"I can make all those with Item Creation! Leave it to me!"

"So you *are* just making fun of me?!"

The girls were already hard at work making stuff, and he wanted to stop them, but—"Hee-hee, Ma-kun!" "Let go!"—Mamako wasn't ready to release him from her embrace.

"A-anyway, that's all over with, so you should really do your paperwork! Okay, Mom?"

"Oh, right! I'll be right back!"

Mamako dashed over to the counter and quickly filled out the form they handed her, slipping it in just before the deadline. Whew.

Mamako was given a number, which she tied around her waist. It was 10362.

"Since you're the last person to enter…that means there are 10,362 moms in this thing? That's…a lot."

"Then I'll just go do this prelim thing!"

"And onward to victory!" cheered Wise, followed by well-wishes from Medhi and Porta.

"I'm sure we have no reason to worry at all, Mamako, but do take care."

"Good luck, Mama!"

Still visibly excited, Mamako was led behind the counter: "Now, Mamako, if you would come this way."

Once she was gone, Shiraaase turned toward the children.

"Since we made it here in time, once more, as my name is Shiraaase, and *Shiraaase* means 'infooorm,' I must infooorm you of some things… But where should I begin?"

"No keeping secrets, no entertaining yourself," replied Masato. "Just infooorm us of everything. Although, I think we get the big picture…"

"The World Matriarchal Arts Tournament is a tournament for mothers only, and Mamako was planning on entering," said Wise. "She told us that much!"

"Someone told her to keep it a secret until the day of the tournament…"

"And we think that someone was you, Ms. Shiraaase!"

"Yes, it was."

"Of course…" Masato shot her a baleful glare.

She showed no signs of shame. Her ever-present placidity never wavered.

"The reason I advised her to keep it a secret is simply because I had concerns about your reaction, Masato. While Mamako basks in the limelight, you're left on the sidelines, unable to join in… I imagined you would be bitterly opposed to that."

"Hate to break it to you, but I'm not that childish. There was no need for concern!"

"In hindsight, perhaps not. However, no matter what, I needed to get Mamako to enter the World Matriarchal Arts Tournament. Her participation is absolutely necessary."

Shiraaase held up a hand with three fingers raised.

"To begin, the World Matriarchal Arts Tournament itself has three reasons for existing… The first one is, naturally, the tournament's status as an event. An entertainment spectacle in which mothers of all races compete, and audience members are impressed once again by how magnificent mothers truly are."

"We see how OP mine is on a daily basis, and you want to show us how strong *other* moms are… Ugh…"

"And no one would care about a mom tournament if Mamako wasn't in it. She's famous, and apparently tons of other moms wanna fight her. So what's the second thing?" asked Wise.

"The second reason is strategic—we're hoping to lure out the forces that don't think highly of mothers."

"The Libere Rebellion— They'll definitely attend to mess up a mom-only event," said Medhi. "And you need Mamako's ultimate power to ambush them… Right?"

"Ultimately, we're hoping Mamako, the other mothers, and all of you will help turn the tables and totally beat the snot out of them."

"Working together to dominate our foes… Just the idea makes me excited," Medhi gushed, her beautiful face reddening.

"Hey, Wise…" "Yeah, no need to remind me." Medhi's dark power may be frightening, but she was in their party. The hero's party.

And then Porta's hand shot up.

"Ms. Shiraaase! There's one reason left! What is it?"

"Very well. The third reason…" Shiraaase stared at the three fingers she held up for a long moment, thinking.

Then she lowered one of the fingers.

"Forgive me, there were only two reasons. I was mistaken when I said there were three."

"No, no, that wasn't a mistake!" shouted Masato. "You just chose not to tell us the last one!"

"I bet you were thinking 'It'll be more interesting if they don't know!'" said Wise.

"You misunderstand me. There are two reasons to hold the World Matriarchal Arts Tournament. But beyond those…we want Mamako participating in case the unexpected happens."

"You think something other than a Rebellion attack might happen?"

"Let us say the chance exists. At the current time, as an admin, I can say nothing more definite… Let's say you should keep the possibility of a third reason in the corner of your mind. The main point is that this tournament has a purpose, and Mamako is required to fulfill that."

She didn't seem like she was messing with them.

Mamako was a key part of their plans. That much made sense.

Masato acquiesced. "Okay. Then we'll go with that for now…"

"So what should we do?" asked Wise.

"We don't have any plans…," said Medhi. "And we were just transported here, so we hardly know our way around town…"

"Should we just wait here for Mama to come back?"

"Hmm… That'd be real boring. I guess we could watch the prelims?" Wise suggested.

But Shiraaase shook her head.

"I'm afraid they aren't open to the public. There are too many participants, and staff can't monitor everything. To avoid stealthy support from the mothers' fan bases, we've been forced to bar them from entering."

"Oh… Well, I guess it's good to keep things fair. But now I kinda wanna watch… Your admin rights can't do anything about this?" Wise asked, her eyes sparkling.

Shiraaase's mind was as unflappable as her expression, so this was likely a wasted effort.

No, maybe not. Shiraaase did seem to be thinking about it. "Hmm… Well, I can't say there *aren't* ways for you to watch the prelims."

"So we can watch them?" asked Medhi. "Could you please tell us how?"

"I'd like to know how! I want to see Mama fight!"

"Wise, Medhi, Porta… I understand how you feel. However…"

"Er, uh… It's not like I'm worried about her or anything, but sure."

Masato raised his hand, but not very high. Making it clear he wasn't enthusiastic.

"I see that all of you, Masato included, would like to watch. Very well. Let me explain how… The tournament office is accepting applications for volunteer staff. That is all."

A very simple explanation, but it sufficed.

"So if we're staff, we can go in and out of the venue as we please," said Masato, to which Wise pointed out, "But we'd also have to do our jobs."

"And there's a possibility we'll be asked to do some very dangerous jobs," said Medhi.

"If the Rebellion shows up, that would be our responsibility!" added Porta.

"We would certainly ask for your help. But just to be clear, depending on how they choose to act, even if we discover a Rebellion member, we may ask you to monitor the situation instead."

Masato responded to Shiraaase: "So rather than immediately handle them, take a wait-and-see approach… Yeah, makes sense. If we attack suddenly, there'd be collateral damage."

And if they used a dark item to brainwash NPCs?

A stampede of over 10,000 mothers…was something best not thought about.

"R-right. If we spy any Rebellion members, we won't engage."

"Although, I could easily chain cast them into oblivion."

"A shame I can't just bop them on the head, but if those are our orders…"

"I can keep a promise!"

"Thank you," said Shiraaase. "This way, please."

She handed them staff badges on lanyards.

Masato's party became volunteer staff!
"And Wise can no longer use magic."

"Such a shame this always happens…"

"Wise! Here's an item that removes Seal!"

"*Sniff…* I'm so sorry, you guys… Yeah, like hell I am! Our occupations didn't even change, so I can still use magic just fine!"

""…Awww…"" Disappointment.

"Hey! Masato?! Medhi?! Why is that a problem?!"

They'd reached the point where they didn't even want their Sage using magic.

Shiraaase got their paperwork done up, and they were immediately put on cleaning duty.

Carrying brooms and dustpans, they entered the tournament hall. They moved toward the large indoor arena where the prelims were held, sweeping the halls as they went.

"Shiraaase has executive committee work to do, so she went off somewhere and left us doing odd jobs…while Mom's a contestant in this tournament. Once again, I've proven to have no value…"

"Quit whining and get to sweeping. Honestly, this is ideal," commented Wise. "They didn't specify where to clean, so we can clean where we like."

"But I think we should avoid spending too much time in the prelim hall. I mean, it is Mamako…," said Medhi.

"And she'll see Masato right away, get all excited, and develop some amazing skill!" gushed Porta.

"Ugh, probably. And if the officials think we're secretly assisting her, she might get disqualified… We'd better watch from a distance, making sure she doesn't notice." *She can be a real pain*, Masato groaned to himself as the group went around the building's perimeter. "If only there were windows… Oh, there's one!" Exactly where they needed it.

They peeked inside—it definitely looked like the prelim arena. There were a number of different battle stages set up, and crowds of mothers with numerous spectators gathered around, from fairies the size of your palm to giants towering over fifteen feet tall. They could watch safely from here.

But the window was a little high.

"We can see just fine, but Porta's a bit out of luck…"

"Awww… I wanna see…"

"Masato, let her sit on your shoulders," Wise ordered.

"Or get down on your hands and knees and let her stand on you," suggested Medhi.

Let a twelve-year-old sit on your shoulders or let her use you as a stool. The choice was obvious.

"Go ahead, step on me."

""""Wha—?""""

"Uh, just kidding! That was a joke! Shoulder seat it is!"

Masato definitely wasn't into getting stepped on by little girls. Not at all! Honest!

Anyway.

"Porta, shoulder docking!"

"Yes! I have docked with Masato!"

Porta had held out both arms sideways; he'd hefted her up and placed her on his shoulders.

"Well, Porta? Can you see now?"

"Yes! I can see perfectly!"

"Think you could go a little lower, though? Everyone on that side can see Porta easily; they might catch us looking," noted Wise.

"Masato, can you duck down a bit?" asked Medhi. "A bit more? More than that."

"S-sure…"

He knelt down so Porta's face was level with Wise's and Medhi's at the base of the windowsill.

And found himself staring at the wall.

"Oh no! If I'm on his shoulders, Masato can't see inside!"

"No, that's fine… As long as you can see, Porta, I don't mind. I'm mildly curious about Mom's battle, but…I'm receiving something far more precious here."

Specifically, Masato's face was gently pinned between Porta's… No, let's not go there. Masato's not that kind of guy! Really!

"But since I can't see, can you give me a running commentary on what's going on?"

"There's a staff member onstage, explaining things...," Wise began. "Oh, they just started lining up kitchen counters on the stage. Lots of vegetables. Seems like the prelim round is cooking."

"Well, it is a mom tournament. Makes sense they'd compete in housework... Is there anyone who looks like they could give Mom a run for her money?"

Medhi took over: "Let's see... There's a beastkin sharpening her claws, and a ninja with her own set of knives, and an android equipped with some sort of laser blade... They look strong."

"Not your typical cooking-competition lineup... A-and not that I care, but what's Mom up to?"

"She's not onstage yet!" replied Porta. "They started with number one, and it looks like they'll be competing in order! It's going to be a very long wait!"

"Oh, okay... Right, she's got, like, over ten thousand people ahead of her..."

Then he was going to be waiting here like this, with Porta on his shoulders, for a very long time. It was definitely taking its toll on his back and knees already. But the blissful feelings around his neck made it all okay...

While his mind was in the gutter, however:

"...Wait, should we even be doing this?" Wise asked, sounding uncharacteristically serious.

"Where'd that come from? You're the one who said we should watch the prelims in the first place."

"Yeah, I know, but..."

"This tournament is just bait to lure out the enemies," Medhi chimed in.

Wise nodded. "Mothers gather from around the world, joining in this massive tournament... They've got to come. I was talking big in front of Shiraaase, but honestly, if we're the only line of defense, we're in big trouble. If we fight them head-on, it won't end well."

"They're the kind of people that plant bombs all over town, force parents and children to fight one another— They show no mercy. And the Four Heavenly Kings of the Libere Rebellion don't just have awful personalities and attitudes—they've got really dangerous skills. It's absolutely possible all of them will attack at once, too…"

"Urp… I'm getting kinda scared now…," whimpered Porta.

The excitement of peeking into the prelims drained away. All eyes stared anxiously at the floor.

This called for a word from their leader, the hero, Masato.

"Amante, who backs up her incredible physical stats with a skill that reflects all damage. Sorella, who can control a million undead monsters at once and has a mega-powerful debuff skill that craters all her opponents' stats. And there are two more like that… Ha-ha, not happening! They're not just gonna show up out of nowhere! We can relax! Ha-ha!"

The cheer was forced, a desperate attempt to dispel his party's fears.

And just then:

"Argh, you guys *again*?!"

"Ew. Why are theyyy here?!"

The voices came from behind: one hyper-aggressive, the other thick with disgust. Both female.

The party spun around, but there was only one person behind them.

A very large…human? Well over six feet tall, completely covered by a silver robe with a mask, like a member of some secret magic society.

Deeply suspicious. And kinda scary.

"Yikes?! Who the…?"

"I-intruders!"

"That's the most suspicious person I've ever seen! Report this at once!"

"Actually, I think the way we were peeking at the prelims was pretty suspicious, too!"

""""Oh… Good point, Porta.""""

This last exchange helped calm everyone down.

Looking closely, this new arrival had a number: 3782. While certainly alarming-looking, this meant they were a participating mother.

With Porta still on his shoulders, Masato hastily straightened and showed his staff badge.

"Um, we're tournament staff! Not intruders or anything! We were just sneaking a quick peek at the prelim progress."

"O-oh, cool. Didn't expect you to explain all politely..."

"Seems like they haven't guessed our real identityyyy. Mwa-ha-haaa."

"Er... What identity? And why are there two voices? Are there two of you in there?"

"Yep. Since I'm the stronger one, I've gotta carry this gamble-holic lady around..."

"Stoppp! Stopppp! There's only one person in heeere! ...You, down there, don't say another wooord! Talking is my jooob! You are not allowed to explaaain!"

An argument appeared to be taking place inside the masked robe. There were definitely two people in there.

And both voices sounded familiar. Maybe...just maybe...

Yeah... It's definitely them.

He was sure of it.

Masato wanted to ask them directly, but before he could...

"Oh my! I thought that was you, Ma-kun!"

...the window behind them opened, and Mamako poked out her head.

"Yikes! Mom?!"

"That's right; it's Mommy! I saw just a bit of Ma-kun's hair and went *Wait, is thaaat...?* and came running over, and it *was* you! Hee-hee."

"You can identify me from my hair alone?! What sort of terrifying skill is that?! Also, we're kinda busy right now... Huh?"

The suspicious mother was no longer behind him.

He looked around and spied them bent backward like a giant shrimp, running very fast, a shriek trailing in their wake.

The entire party frowned, looking at one another.

"...You thinking what I'm thinking?"

"Yep," agreed Wise. "Don't even say it out loud. That was definitely those two."

"The fact that we were legitimately afraid of anyone who would take such a ridiculously stupid approach to getting in here really ticks me off," Medhi fumed. "Makes me want to punch them right now."

"Cool, I approve."

"Go get 'em."

"B-but…we promised Ms. Shiraaase we'd monitor the situation!"

"Oh, right…," said Masato. "Then I guess we can let 'em go for now…"

"Goodness, what are you all talking about? Ma-kun, fill Mommy in? Please?"

Mamako tried getting his attention, but his mind was on other things.

Masato felt the tension drain out of him. He let out a long sigh.

And it was finally time for Mamako's prelim.

Looking quite nervous, the staff member in charge announced, "And finally, will entry number 10362 please step onstage?"

"Okay! Thank you!"

The prelim challenge: make a salad.

Contestants used the vegetables piled on the counters onstage, the prep speed and degree of completion affected their overall score, and the top sixteen names would advance to the main competition.

Mamako took the stage, and a hush fell over the hall.

Humans, elves, beastkin, angels and devils alike—all mothers present turned to watch, not wishing to miss a moment of Mamako's performance. She was under a lot of pressure.

But Mamako was still Mamako. She just had to make a tasty dish, as she always did, with her precious children's health in mind.

"The salads we're making double as consolation prizes, so we can bring them home with us. That'll be one part of tonight's dinner… What should I do for the main dish? I wonder what Ma-kun would like?"

Mamako drew her swords as she contemplated the evening menu.

Terra di Madre in her right, Altura in her left. Using her Holy Swords as kitchen utensils.

"Time to begin! Ready…start!"

"Hyah!"

At the signal, Mamako swung Altura. The water-powered Holy Sword sent forth a stream of water, washing the vegetables while lifting them into the air.

"And then, *hyah!*"

She swung Terra di Madre, and countless stone blades shaped like kitchen knives sprang out of the counter, chopping all the veggies. Perfectly chopped, they fell…

…onto a plate: lettuce, cabbage, red cabbage, carrots, and tomatoes.

A fresh veggie salad, colorful and vibrant!

Prep time from start to finish: one second.

"Now, what should I do for the dressing? Hee-hee."

"W-wow… Mamako—no, contestant 10362—has placed first in the prelims!"

There was a momentary silence, then a thunderous round of applause. "That's Mamako Oosuki's true power…" "It's overwhelming!" "We have witnessed the power of the world's strongest mother!" Holding their own take-home salads, many mothers stood in awe of her skills.

Meanwhile…

…in the shadows, two pairs of eyes glared balefully at Mamako through the face and belly of a masked robe.

"Already taking first place… *Tch*, saw it coming."

"It is just a preliiiim. And we passed the prelim, tooooo. All according to plaaan. We just have to beat her while everyone's waaatching."

"Yeah. We can do it… We'll show her the power of the Four Heavenly Kings of the Libere Rebellion!"

They cast aside the silver-masked robe, and beneath it…were two girls.

Anti-mom Amante, she who rejects the concept of mothers, radiating hostility like a wild tiger.

Scorn-mom Sorella, she who scorns all mothers, fingers twirling in her dubiously colored hair, eyes gazing languidly down.

Sorella was riding on Amante's shoulders.

Just like Porta had ridden on Masato's shoulders.

"We went through so much trouble to get here… Learning about the tournament before it began, making plans to infiltrate undetected… staying up all night sewing this robe to disguise our identities…"

"No need to explain our tearstained efforts to meeee. Running into Masato's party like that was a bluuunder. But they didn't know who we weeeere. And the prelims are oooover. Let's just go hooome. We've seen Mamako in action, so our goals have been accoooomplished."

"Yeah. We confirmed Mamako Oosuki's participation. But…if I could just find one more…"

Amante squinted, peering around the crowd of moms.

There were just too many mothers here. Too many races and types; it was next to impossible to locate any one individual.

"The master said there was a mysterious being here, neither a test player nor an NPC… But I dunno who that could be."

"Well, if they were so weak they failed at the preliiims, who caaares? Stiiiill… If they manage to make it into the main rouuund…"

"Then we'll take them and Mamako Oosuki down."

"Exaaactly. For now, retreeeat! We must make secret preparations to wiiin!"

"Yep. Let's go… This is our chance to show the power of the Libere Rebellion. We'll use this tournament as proof that the age of mothers is over!"

A secret declaration of war.

Amante and Sorella turned to leave the prelim hall unnoticed. "Ah! We've got to wear the robe!" "They'll guess who we aaaare!" The two sinister villains hastily put their disguise back on.

ELF
MAMAKO

SKILLS

FOOD CULTIVATION
Using a traditional elf Food Source, she can obtain food anywhere, at any time.

CLOTHES-HANGER TREES
Can cultivate trees that move on their own in search of sunlight. Laundry hung on these dries well.

STRENGTHS

Her superior ingredient acquisition ability means she never has to worry about her next meal.

WEAKNESSES

Since elves live in settlements secluded from the rest of the world, she struggles with going into town to shop. And no matter how wonderful her pointy elf ears are, she's still Masato's actual mother, so he doesn't seem very happy about them.

STATS

STATS

MATERNITY: 100 / COOKING: 120 / LAUNDRY: 100
CLEANING: 80 / SHOPPING: 60 / COMBAT: 100
MA-KUN: 100

SPECIAL   HOLINESS: 100

Chapter 2 The Way of the Mother Teaches the Art of Using the Body and Tools to Do Housework...Apparently.

Soft shouts echoed across the inn's garden.

"Hah! And... Yah! Rah!"

The morning sunlight made Firmamento, the Holy Sword of the Heavens, sparkle.

The morning power put wind in the sails of Masato's practice swings.

"Humph... Good enough for today."

One last dramatic swing, and his morning training was complete.

"Not often do I wake up early enough to practice like this...but it's pretty heroic of me. I'm really starting to embody this whole hero thing. Soon all shall know I'm the hero. Mwa-ha-ha."

After indulging himself with this fantasy, it was time to do something about all this sweat.

Masato put away the sword and went inside, down the hall to the bath.

"Man, my body's in top shape now! Just look at these biceps. Buff as heck. Mwa-ha-ha."

Standing in his underwear in the changing room, he flexed a few times, admiring the results, then took off his underwear, flexed again, went into the spacious bath, and flexed some more, thoroughly satisfied with himself.

After one more flex, it was time to wash his hair. Just as he had shampoo bubbles everywhere...

"Mm?"

...he sensed someone behind him.

A moment later, something extremely soft pressed up against his back. "Wha—?!" And whoever that was pressed up against him began to massage his scalp.

Both the sensation on his back and the hands on his head felt familiar.

This was definitely a mom shampoo. With all the soap, he couldn't open his eyes to see, but he was sure.

You could search the whole world over and only find one person who would do this to him!

"Hey, Mom! What the heck?!"

His protests were basically a reflex at this point.

"I'm just bringing you some towels! It's almost time for breakfast, so don't take too long!"

Mamako's voice came from the changing room.

Not from behind him.

"Uh… Wait, what?"

He quickly dumped some water on his head, rinsing away the shampoo.

And when he turned around—

"……………Huh?"

—no one was there.

"I could've sworn that was my mom… But she was in the changing room. Then who was washing my hair? I definitely felt it, so it couldn't have been a ghost… Hmm…"

Masato left the bathroom to investigate.

The party was staying at an inn set aside for mothers participating in the tournament and those affiliated with them. The interior design was certainly upscale, with an elegance that definitely made it feel more luxurious than the inns they usually stayed at.

Masato was outside the girls' room. He knocked once, then opened the door and peeked in.

"*Zzzz… Mmph…*"

Wise was lying there, sprawled out like she was in the middle of some bizarre dance—typical—belly and panties partially on display.

"…Mm…mm…" *Poke, poke.*

Medhi was lying next to her, breathing peacefully but prodding Wise with her staff in her sleep.

"Mmph... I wanna...cheer...for Mama... *Zzz...*"

Porta appeared to be trying her best, even in her dreams.

All three girls were still sound asleep.

"From the way those things felt, only Medhi was even a remote possibility..."

But she was still out cold. It didn't seem at all possible she'd given Masato a shampoo, come running back here, and was now pretending to sleep.

Porta and Wise were ruled out based on size alone.

"So... What the heck? *Was* it Mom? ...Huh. I don't get it."

Had the mom shampooing him been Mamako's afterimage? A ninja art? A clone?

All seemed unlikely...so the only remaining option was to ask her.

"Mom's probably getting breakfast ready. I'll check there."

The tournament committee had rented out the entire inn, but the inn's staff were absent. Guests had to do their own cooking and laundry.

Mothers participating in the tournament were all housework experts, so taking care of these things was like an easy warm-up. Supposedly.

"No matter what inn we stay at, Mom ends up doing the laundry and cooking herself...even when she's got a tournament to win."

He left the room and went down the hall, lured by the smell of breakfast.

Someone must have been chopping pickled vegetables; he could hear the *tok-tok-tok* of a knife on a cutting board.

A familiar sound: his mother at work.

Masato stepped into the dining room, took a seat at the table, and called out to her:

"Hey, Mom, question for you."

Mamako, working in the kitchen, called back...

"Oh my! I have a son? I had no idea! *Hee-hee-hee.*"

"...Huh?"

No—that wasn't her usual voice. It was certainly every bit as kind as Mamako's voice, but there was something off about it.

"Er, huh? ...You're...not my mom?"

Masato turned toward the kitchen.

The woman standing there was dressed in grass-green clothes, like a hunter. She had long blond hair...

...and long, pointy ears.

"Oh! ...A-are you...an elf?!"

"Yes! I'm an elf."

The woman turned around. Taut features, long and narrow eyes, those distinctive pointed ears—definitely a female elf.

As Masato stood there stunned, the girls came filing into the dining room.

"*Yaaawn*... Yo, Masato, it's too early for you to be yelling like— Huh? Who's that?!"

"An elf...?"

"Um... G-good morning!"

"Yes, it is a lovely morning. Wise, Medhi, Porta, Masato...I see everyone's up! I'd better hurry and finish breakfast!"

The elf lady gave them all a gentle smile and went back to her cooking.

She seemed so busy, they hesitated to say more.

"Um...," started Masato. "I hate to interrupt, but..."

"What is it? Oh, yes! I haven't introduced myself! My name is Chaliele. I'm an elf mother. Nice to meet you!"

"Chaliele... Nice to meet you, too."

"So if you're an elf mom, and you're here at this inn," said Wise, "you must be...?"

"Part of the World Matriarchal Arts Tournament?" asked Medhi.

"That's right! I came in second in the prelims. One step behind Mamako!"

"Amazing! You're Mama's rival!"

"So, Chaliele, what are you doing here?" Masato asked her. "It sounded like you knew us..."

"I'm staying at this inn, too. And I heard all about you from Mamako! I met her earlier, and we got to talking...and since we're all pressed for time, we decided to split up the housework."

She'd been cooking through their entire conversation, but now she paused.

"Hmm… I don't think I've got enough ingredients."

"Oh, then should I run out and buy something?" offered Masato.

"My, how nice of you! Thanks for offering! But don't worry. I thought this might happen, so I came prepared."

Chaliele reached into her pocket and pulled out a few small paper parcels.

"This is an elf mother's secret weapon: a Food Source. You use it like this…"

First, she opened the bundle with a drawing of a mushroom on it. Inside was a powder. She took a pinch of this and sprinkled it on the cutting board…

…and a bunch of tasty-looking mushrooms grew out of it!

Next was a bundle with peas on it. A pinch of powder, scattered on the kitchen's mud walls, and…

Buds grew out of the wall, stems rising, flowers blooming, and a number of pea pods appeared!

"As you can see, elf mothers can get ingredients whenever they need them!"

"Wow!" marveled Wise. "Growing your own ingredients in the kitchen and cooking them as you harvest! That's nuts…"

"I can see why you placed so highly… You're a kitchen powerhouse," said Medhi, followed by Porta and Masato: "Amazing! What a surprise!" "That's definitely quite the skill…"

"I'll just grow some more! That way, all of you can eat your fill."

Chaliele opened all the other packets, sprinkling powder on the floor and pillars. The room was soon filled with different types of beans and mushrooms, and the kitchen was overflowing with natural ingredients.

Observing all this, Masato frowned.

Definitely amazing, but that's gonna be hell to clean up…

But as he watched the kitchen vanish under the vegetation, he decided not to mention it.

Mamako finished the laundry and joined them, and it was time to eat.

Set atop the table were rice and peas, mushroom miso soup, boiled potatoes, and a salad of pickled veggies. A healthy menu, full of the natural ingredients elves took such pride in.

On one side sat the elf mother, Mamako, and Porta.

On the other: Wise, Masato, and Medhi.

Everyone helped themselves as soon as they took their seats.

"This is my first time eating elf food," said Masato. "I wonder what it's like? I can't wait!"

"I hope you all enjoy it…"

"My tongue's gotten used to Mamako's cooking, so it's pretty picky! All right… Let's start with the soup! Here goes!" Wise often claimed miso soup had vital MP restoration powers.

Chaliele watched nervously as she took a sip.

"Hmm… It's…pretty dang good!"

The verdict: PASS!

"Definitely a different stock than Mamako uses, but I like it!"

"We make the stock from kelp that grows in the mountains, not the sea. It's quite common in elf settlements but I imagine not widely used by other races."

"Yeah? Then I'd better try some, too…" Masato took a sip. "Wow, it is really good. No arguments from me."

Porta chimed in, "I agree! It goes perfectly with the peas and rice!"

"I can see why you qualified for the main tournament," said Medhi. "Mamako has a serious rival already."

"Oh yeah. That's right. They're being friendly and divvying up the chores, but…Mom and Chaliele might have to fight later."

As he spoke, he quietly activated his skill, A Child's Sense. Just to make sure—and to measure her potency.

When he glanced across the table…he saw Mamako and Chaliele bathed in carnation-colored light. This red color was proof of mother-hood. They were definitely both mothers.

And both produce about the same volume of light…

How bright a mother glowed was a sign of how powerful a mother she was. Which meant…

…unless her race could freely adjust their degree of motherhood, they were roughly evenly matched.

"Mom, you can't let your guard down against Chaliele."

"That is true. Hee-hee. Mommy's so excited!" She smiled.

"I'm looking forward to it myself! I'm not about to let Mamako win!" Chaliele smiled, too.

Both mothers wore matching gentle grins. "Doesn't seem like they're ever going to fight..." The mood definitely contained no promise of blood-drenched mortal combat in their future.

Then Wise spoke up.

"Oh, hey, I was wondering... Should we really be eating *all* of this? What about your kids, Chaliele?"

This question drew a sad smile from Chaliele.

"Don't worry about it. My child isn't here with me... She left the settlement a long time ago, and I have no idea where she is."

"Oh my goodness!" exclaimed Mamako. "I had no idea. You must be so worried!"

"I just wish she'd told me more before she left. All I know is that she went to the capital of Catharn to join someone's party..."

"The capital of Catharn? Didn't we...?"

That was the first place Masato and Mamako had gone after entering the game and where they'd first met Wise and Porta.

And come to think of it...

Huh? Didn't we meet an elf, too...?

They definitely had.

An elf girl had applied to join Masato's party.

Her name was Salite. Nineteen, in human years. An elf priestess who dedicated her life to prayer, the type of deeply religious person you definitely wanted to avoid.

Unfortunately, she had failed to pass Mamako's mom interview...

"...Um, Chaliele, what's your daughter like?"

"Well...if I do say so myself, she's a wonderful girl. Sincere, thoughtful, gets along with everybody. I'm very proud of her."

"Oh... If she's that sociable, then I guess I'm thinking of the wrong elf."

"Also, her name's Salite. She's nineteen in human years."

"Pfffft?!"

Miso soup sprayed everywhere. "Ma-kun! Are you all right?" "Uh, yeah, I'm fine." "I'm a lot less fine!" The spray had shot in the direction of Wise, but everyone else was unharmed. Whew.

A miso-soaked Sage punched Masato hard in the shoulder, but he was used to that by now.

"Uh, Chaliele? You don't know anything else? Like, her current job or…any religious affiliations?"

"I haven't heard from her, so I can't say…but I'm sure she's fine. She has a good head on her shoulders."

"I…I see…"

For better or worse, Chaliele was unaware of her daughter's current status.

Which meant he had better watch out for Mamako.

If Mom figures it out and says something weird, it could mean trouble!

It was Mamako who stamped a failure mark on Chaliele's daughter at that interview.

She had good reasons for it, but Chaliele knew none of that and would hardly be pleased to hear about it. She'd be upset. She might even get downright angry.

The moment she found out about the interview results, things between them would start to fester.

Was there a risk that this pleasant competition could turn into a tragic blood feud?!

He had to ensure this stayed secret!

"Ma-kun, what's wrong? You've gone white as a sheet! Are you feeling sick?"

"No!! No, I'm fine!! Never better!! …Uh…Chaliele! I hope you find your daughter…maybe not soon but…sometime after the tournament's over!"

"Yes, that's my hope. By joining this tournament, I hope news of me will spread across the world, and she'll see it and come back home. That's the main reason I decided to join in. Hee-hee!"

"Oh, then you simply must do your very best. I certainly will be! Hee-hee!"

Both mothers grinned, vowing to fight the good fight. Mamako seemed to have entirely forgotten Salite.

Meanwhile, Wise and Porta hadn't noticed either—and Medhi hadn't joined the party until much later.

Only Masato was left with a stomachache.

At least we got through that safely... Let's hope we can keep the peace. Lord! Hear my plea!

In his mind's eye, he clasped his hands, offering up a fervent prayer.

There was something he'd meant to ask Mamako, but he had completely forgotten about it.

Once everyone was ready, it was time to set out.

"Make sure you haven't forgotten anything!"

"Yeah, only moms need to check that stuff? We're not actually in the tournament..."

"Oh, hang on! We're volunteer staff!"

"We mustn't forget our staff badges. We need those to abuse our positions and observe the matches from a location far better than the stands. Where are those badges?"

"Don't worry! I've got all our badges! Here you go!"

"Sounds like everyone's ready. As am I!" Chaliele had a grass-green leather bag on her back.

"Right, then—"

""Let's go! Yay!""

"I knew you'd interrupt me. Didn't think it would be both of you at once! *Moms!*"

With the mothers leading the way, the party moved out and headed down the wide road from the inn to the tournament hall.

They might have to fight today, but Mamako and Chaliele seemed super-relaxed. They were chattering away like friends whose kids had grown up together.

Meanwhile, the children following them were all looking pretty tense.

"Geez... They are waaaay too chill about this," grumbled Masato.

"With true power comes great aplomb," remarked Wise. "I'm kinda jealous... Us, on the other hand..."

"We can't afford to let our guard down, not after discovering two of the Four Heavenly Kings of the Libere Rebellion," said Medhi. "They may have chosen a very silly way of infiltrating, but they remain a threat."

"I've prepared a lot of recovery items! Leave that to me!"

"As if that wasn't enough, I have my own stuff to worry about... *Sigh*, I'm already tired." Masato flicked the badge hanging from his neck, scanning his surroundings.

The street was crowded. Humans, elves, beastkin, giants, fairies, androids—all sorts of fantasy races, all headed toward the tournament hall. The vast majority must have been spectators. There were staff working as guides here and there, ensuring a smooth flow of foot traffic.

There were a lot of eyes on them. Naturally. Mamako was the biggest name in the tournament.

But the hero—me—hardly has any presence to speak of... Ha-ha...

The thought made him want to cry, so he put it out of his mind.

The more he looked around, the more eyes he accidentally met, so he elected to keep his gaze facing straight ahead.

This gave him an excellent view of Chaliele's pointy ears.

Elf ears... I do like them... Wonder what they feel like...

He must have stared a little too long, because Chaliele stopped and turned toward him.

"You find my ears interesting, Masato?"

"Er? Uh, um... Well, yes. I guess I can admit to being super-curious."

"I see. Then go ahead and touch them."

"You mean it?!"

"Yes, I don't mind...on the condition that you become *my* son. Hee-hee."

"Whaaaaaat?!"

This cry of surprise came not from Masato, but from Mamako.

"Chaliele?! H-h-how could Ma-kun become *your* son?!"

"Quite literally. After all, Masato offered to help with the cooking, and here he is coming to cheer you on in the tournament! He's such a good boy... Masato, what do you say? Do you want to be my son?"

"I..."

"Ma-kun! Ma-kun, Ma-kun, Ma-kun! Can we talk?"

Before Masato could say a word, Mamako pulled him close.

She brushed her hair back, showing him her ear.

"Well, Ma-kun? Mommy's ears! See?!"

"So what? The heck is—?"

She was pushing up against him, ears front and center.

The girls all shook their heads.

"Come *on*, Masato! Take a hint!" said Wise, exasperated. "Chaliele's invitation made Mamako jealous!"

"Huh? Jealous?! Of what?!"

"How can anyone be so dense...? This is bad news. Mamako's unleashed the special mom skill A Mother's Envy—a charge skill. Once she stores up enough jealousy, she unleashes a powerful technique—"

"Yo, Medhi...can you stop making stuff up? There is no such skill."

"I'm not so sure! This is Mama we're talking about!"

"Urk... Th-that's true... As long as we're talking about my mom, literally anything is possible... Still..."

"See, Ma-kun?! Mommy's ears? Well? Do you like them?!" *Shove, shove.*

"Arghhh! Knock it off! I don't—"

But before he could say he didn't care...

"You must be Mamako Oosuki! I've found you at last!"

...a woman's voice interrupted, shouting over him. Or maybe a mother's?

A shadow was racing across the roofs that lined the street, moving so fast, all they could see was a blur. "And *hup!*" she shouted, leaping with superhuman strength and landing in front of the party.

She looked exactly like any other middle-aged woman.

But she had a fluffy tail and animal ears. They appeared to be canine.

She was carrying five young children in slings: three on her back, one on each side.

"Most people would have hurt themselves falling from that height, but you made it look effortless...," marveled Masato. "Who are you...?"

"I'm a beastkin mom! And—!"

But before she could continue: "Yay!" "She jumped!" "Wow!" "Do it again!" "Please!" Her children started kicking up a fuss, tiny tails wagging. They looked like a boisterous bunch.

"Yes, yes, later, okay? Mom's gotta talk to these people now. You there, girls with the staff badges—you're with the tournament, right? I'm gonna leave the little ones with you."

""""Huh?"""""

While Wise stood stunned—"Waaait?!"—two kids were foisted off on her, followed by two on Medhi. "No warning?!" And one on Porta. "Whoa!" No protests were heeded.

"Whew… Got that taken care of. Now, where are my manners?"

The beastkin mother faced Mamako…

But then—

"Oh, it's Mamako Oosuki! I simply must say hello!"

—a water spout shot up from the corner, and a giant ball of water was flung upward…

…scoring a direct hit on Masato. "Hey, you could've killed me!!" But it was actually surprisingly soft; he was unharmed.

The ball was too large for him to really get his arms around it; and inside was a fantastical creature. The upper half was a human woman, and the lower half, a fish.

And a pouch with a child inside was hanging in front of her.

"Now, I'm probably wrong here, but…you must be a *shishamo*-with-child mermaid… Nah, that would just be ridiculous! Ah-ha-ha—!"

"No, you're right! I *am* a *shishamo* mermaid, and I am a mother with a child!"

"You've gotta be kidding me…"

"Oh, you there, the staff girl in red. Nice timing! I need to talk to Mamako Oosuki for a minute, so can you hold my child?"

"Huh? Wha—?! Me?! Wait, hold up! I'm not on day care duty! I'm not even good at it! Like, I learned my lesson last time, but… Hey… Augh!"

With two beastkin children already latched onto her, Wise now found herself holding a mermaid child. "*Blub, blub!*" it squealed. "Ack, it's all wiggly!" Wise had been slapped twice by its little tail already. It was kinda funny.

But then…

"I do beg your pardon! I almost got crushed there!"

…a tiny person crawled out of Masato's shirt pocket, wearing a hat made from a flower. "Wha—? How? When did you…?!" It was a fairy woman about the size of his palm, with butterfly wings on her back. And she had a kid, too.

"Mommy's going to go greet her rival. You stay with this day care lady and be good, okay?"

"Okay! Bye-bye, Mommy!"

"Day care lady... What?! Me?!"

The thumb-sized child fairy took a seat on Medhi's head. That was settled.

And then...

"Wow! Mamako Oosuki! It's a mom meet and greet!"

...the earth shook, and a massive mom and child came skipping over. The mother giant towered over fifteen feet tall, and her little girl over nine. The mother seemed rather thickheaded.

"Mommy's gonna say hi, 'kay? You be nice to the day care people!"

"Got it! Hey, tiny lady! Let's play!"

"Eep?! Am I the tiny lady?!"

Porta was only a little over four feet tall, but now she was babysitting a giant more than twice her size. "Let's play!" "O-okay! I can play!" But she was still trying her best—such a good girl.

By this time, the crowd was absurd. Everyone was talking at once.

"How many of them are...? Augh! Not another one!"

They were still coming. More and more of them.

A brilliant magic circle appeared in the sky, and an angel clutching a child descended toward them.

Darkness spewed out of the gap between two buildings, and a devil appeared in a sexy, far too revealing outfit.

In the distance, a dragon attacked. Above their heads were what looked like a dragonewt mother and child.

A sudden puff of smoke nearby, and a ninja with a child appeared. What now...?

"I'm sure they're all mothers appearing in the tournament... They're all trying to greet Mom, apparently. In that case..."

Mamako needed to greet them and settle down this mess. Right!

"Mom! Only way to stop this madness is if you—"

"Hey, Ma-kun! Mommy's ears! See?! You can touch them!" *Shove, shove.*

"You're *still* doing that?! This isn't the time!"

Mamako remained in a fit of jealousy, oblivious to the swarm of mothers around them.

He clearly had to handle this outburst of envy first. There was only one thing to do.

Masato put his fingers on the lobes of Mamako's ears and waggled them.

"Well, Ma-kun, what do you think?"

"Uh, sure, sure. They feel fine. Mom's ears." *Waggle.*

"That's right! These are your mommy's ears! Don't ever forget them!"

"Yeah, yeah, I know. Feeling better now? Time we moved forward. Come on!"

"Oh, Ma-kun…you don't understand how Mommy feels at all… But oh well. I do have a tournament to enter!"

She still seemed a little disgruntled but, shaking such thoughts out of her mind, broke into a run.

She was headed for the back of the tournament hall, the contestant's entrance. This was where the battles would unfold, where the mothers who had attacked them on the road would lie in wait…

And Mamako came running up carrying a towering pile of boxes.

"Sorry to keep you all waiting! First… Everyone who wrote me a letter, if I could just return the favor. My son, Ma-kun, discovered the most wonderful treats! They're just scrumptious!"

"Oh my! How polite! …But wait… I thought I sent you a challenge?"

"Whatever the thoughts behind it, if someone sends you something, you must thank them! That's just good manners! Any mother would do the same."

"And the way she slipped in a humblebrag about her son… There's a mother who has her priorities straight."

"She's already scored a point on all of us. But I won't lose in the real fight! Heh-heh-heh."

All types of mothers gathered, accepting the treat boxes, chattering about this and that...

But Masato had completely lost interest. He was deliberately looking in another direction.

"Where mothers gather, children fear to tread. If I let myself get sucked into that, I'll just regret it."

These moments required children to abuse their status at full throttle, making a great show of apathy.

Time to put his mind on other things.

"The mothers are inside the tournament hall. Now we just have to wait for the matches to begin... What should we do next? As much as I'd love to relax in the stands, we are volunteer staff... Anyone around to explain—er, infooorm us about what work we should be doing?" Masato half joked.

"Ah yes. You rang?"

"Gah?!"

A mysterious nun appeared right next to Masato. "Where did you come from?!" "I was following you closely, yet unobtrusively." Shiraaase had raised being calmly aggravating to an art form.

"In point of fact, I do have a job for you all. Additionally, since I am on the executive committee and quite important, and you are all mere volunteer staff, you have no right to refuse my orders."

"Wow, way to abuse the system... So what do you want?"

"Masato, you join me in the tournament hall. The opening ceremony will begin soon, and I'd like you to participate."

"You need my help with that? Well, I'm sure it's just behind the scenes, so... Fine. I'll do it. Let's go."

Masato started to walk away, but...

"Maaaaaaaasaaaaaaaaaaaatoooooooooooo! You're gonna pay for this!"

...he could have sworn he'd heard Wise's voice from somewhere, tinged with fury.

His imagination? Probably. Yeah. Of course. Masato kept walking.

"Right, time to die... *Spara la magia*—"

"Hey?! No more magic punishments! Calm down!"

Masato hastily spun around and saw…

…Wise, clutching struggling beastkin children under each arm, looking extreeeeemely pissed off.

Next to her was Medhi, holding a thrashing mermaid child in her arms, with a fairy child on her head trying to pull her headband off, looking extreeeeemely stone-faced.

And behind the two of them was Porta, cradled like a doll in the arms of a little-girl giant, looking more like she was the one being babysat, her smile growing ever more strained.

"Masato! You know perfectly well we're in trouble, and you've been ignoring it as hard as you can!"

"You feared if you tried to help at all, you'd get sucked in, so you ran as far from day care duties as you could, abandoning your friends!"

"Er, um… I'd really appreciate some help, too…"

"Sorry! Really sorry! I was only thinking of myself, and I feel very bad about it!"

He was an awful person.

"Look, seriously, I really, really, REALLY can't deal with kids!" Wise yelled. "So stop apologizing and go get someone to help us! NOW! Or I *will* chain cast you to death two thousand times in a row!"

"If you feel even the slightest tinge of genuine contrition, it is your responsibility, your duty to improve this situation as soon as humanly possible," Medhi growled. "If you do not, I have no idea what form my vengeance upon you will take, so I leave that to your wildest imaginings."

"Masato… Please…" Porta sobbed. "Please help us…"

"R-right! Got it! Leave it to me! I'll find a way to save you! By immediately tossing this problem to Shiraaase, with her executive committee privileges!"

"Hmm… It seems the children are rather fond of you. An excellent opportunity to improve your maternal skills… Wise, Medhi, Porta, I leave these children to you."

"""Nooooooooooooooooooooooo!!"""

Shiraaase was the most awful person of all.

Let us lower the curtain before this decision can be overturned.

---

*   *   *

But first...

"Shiraaase's orders, so there's nothing I could do... It's not my fault... Please understand... I genuinely wanted to save you guys! Believe me...!"

Muttering excuses, Masato finished his business and left the staff bathroom.

And found *her* waiting for him in the hall.

"Mm? Uh, Mom?"

At a glance, he addressed her as such, but...

The woman standing there was wearing a black dress.

She was exactly Mamako's height. Her face looked exactly like Mamako's, too, albeit with a much darker expression.

But it wasn't Mamako.

"Oh, sorry... I didn't mean...!" he spluttered, correcting himself. Then he asked, "Uh, um... This area is for staff and contestants only, so...are you in the tournament?"

"........"

The lady in black said nothing. She merely raised a hand.

She touched Masato's hair, straightening it out...and then left without a word.

"Wh-what the...? ...Geez, she looked waaaay too much like Mom..."

He stood staring after her for a moment, then said, "Oh, crap, the ceremony's starting!" He had other priorities. He'd have to think about this later.

The World Matriarchal Arts Tournament main hall, where the chosen mothers would do battle.

At the center of the hall, surrounded by stands, was a rectangular stage with the same kind of wood floors a typical house might have.

Between the stands and the stage was a kid's area, where children could run around and play. This way, the mothers battling onstage could keep an eye on their kids whenever they felt the need, and the children's cheers would reach their ears. It was a layout designed to benefit mothers and children alike. And the childcare staff were always on hand for peace of mind.

Said childcare staff was, of course, the three girls, still mobbed by children.

"Argh! Sure, we might be able to see the matches from the best seats in the house, but I'm still pissed!"

"And we have to look after strangers' children in full view of the public... I can't imagine a harsher trial..."

"Wh-whoa... The whole crowd's staring at us..."

This was a tournament for mothers. Mothers made up a hefty percentage of the crowd. Stern gazes were permanently fixed on Wise, Medhi, and Porta. The girls' battle had already begun.

In the stands was an announcers' booth, and seated inside...were Masato and Shiraaase.

"Um, Shiraaase... Why am I here?"

"To assist with the opening ceremony. Additionally, you will be providing commentary and play-by-play coverage."

"That's an awful lot for an 'additionally'! You can't mean that, right?"

His protest was met with a blank stare. Her eyes still on him...

...Shiraaase turned their mics on.

"Hello, everyone! Thank you for coming. It's finally time for the opening ceremony to begin!"

"Waaaait, you can't start without—!"

"Here come our contestants! A warm round of applause!"

A fanfare echoed through the room, and one by one, contestants began filing onto the stage.

Mamako appeared first.

"Oh my! Such a big crowd— Oh! Ma-kun! You're going to cheer Mommy on from the broadcast booth?! Ma-kun! Maaa-kuuun!" *Yay!*

Mamako began frantically waving her hand at Masato. She was jumping up and down, causing her ample chest to swing all over the place. Bouncing.

"You noticed me way too fast! Calm down! Stop yelling my name!"

"Incidentally, Masato, I also turned on your mic."

"Augh?!"

The son's cry of horror drew a laugh from the stands, and cheers

for Mamako went up from all around. "Mamako!" "Win this thing!" "Good luck to her son, too!" "You guys don't need to cheer for me, too!!" he shrieked. Way too much attention on him already. He was ready to die of shame.

"It's all too much... Please, mercy! Let me be!"

"This is hardly the time to grumble. Masato, your job is to provide commentary. To make things easy, we've provided you a script. This is your job... Nay, your heroic mission."

"Mom gets to be onstage, and the hero reads a script in the broadcast booth... *Sniff...* But fine! Mission accepted!"

Masato stared at the script through his tears and began reading.

"Uh... Th-then let's begin the World Matriarchal Arts Tournament. The main event will follow a standard tournament bracket. Sixteen highly skilled mothers will face one another, aiming for the pinnacle of motherhood."

"The exact nature of each battle will be decided by random draws directly before the event in question," continued Shiraaase. "In addition to normal household tasks like cooking, laundry, and cleaning, some rounds may involve actual combat."

"Then let's begin introducing the contestants. They'll be entering in order following the rankings they achieved in the prelims yesterday. First up is the top-ranked mother from the prelims—"

"Ma-kun's mommy! I'll do my best!" *Yaaay! Yaaay!*

"I said *Calm down!* You're waaay too hyped up! Take a breath!"

"Mamako's reputation precedes her, and we hardly need say more. Masato, the next contestant, please. We have very little time, so make it quick."

"Hurry it up, huh? Got it! Let's get this show on the road!"

Contestant after contestant followed Mamako onstage. He quickly rattled through the introductions.

"Second-ranked! From the sacred forests of the far west, the Sage of the Forest, the elf mother Chaliele!"

"Everyone knows elves, but few know elf mothers— I'll show you our power. Hee-hee."

Pointy ears, blond hair, grass-green clothes—the fantasy classic, mom version.

"Third-ranked! Fire for cooking, water for laundry, earth for cleaning, and wind for shopping... The four elements of housework crystallized in a spirit mother! Etheria!"

"Let's go!" "Okay!" "Now!" "Quadruple spirit fusion!"

Four energy forms gathered together, manifesting in a new form as beautiful as any goddess—quite the fantastical mama.

"Fourth-ranked! A warm, gentle mother's heart in a cold, hard body! Not a child of advanced technology but the mother of it! The android mother! Mechatte!"

"Mother systems all green! Commencing matriarchal mission!"

Trailing a number of high-spec flying drones, a glamorous mechanical mother appeared.

"Fifth-ranked! As the wind blows, as the whim strikes her, before you know it, she's at your side! Don't underestimate our smallest contestant, the fairy mother Nympha!"

"Fortune determines the victor. Like a child who cannot yet predict the outcome. I shall enjoy this."

Flower hat pulled low, blowing bubbles through a pipe, a tiny mother struck an affected pose.

"Sixth-ranked! She's sure she can beat anyone around when it comes to hefting children in her arms! A beastkin mother ready to rampage like a mad-mom! Growlette!"

"Bring on the housework! It's me, the world's number one mom! *Arooo!*"

Her fluffy tail wagging dramatically, the canine beastkin definitely seemed like the plucky sort.

"Seventh-ranked! A mother's role is to support her family from the shadows...like a ninja! Hide a mom's heart beneath this blade, and you get a human mother! Kunoichiko!"

"Today I step out of the shadows and onto the stage! *Nin-nin!*"

She appeared from a puff of smoke. This was a mother determined to keep the whole ninja thing going to the extreme.

"Eighth-ranked! Temptation none can resist will lure victory into her grasp! From the R-rated devil race, a succubus mother! Invi!"

"No need to resist. Come have fun with this sexy mama. Hahhh!"

Her risqué outfit (which was basically just underwear) was enough to enchant just about anyone—this mother was a public indecency charge waiting to happen.

And that was still only half of the contestants.

Masato allowed himself a very small sigh and took a gulp from the glass of water Shiraaase had quietly handed him.

Still eight more to go... This is pretty hard work. Also...

He could see that silver-masked robe waiting to come out next.

"Ahem... Ninth-ranked! Enigmatic...is a nice way of saying deeply suspicious! A human mother! Sorente!"

"Th-th-th-that's not truuuue! We're not suspiciouuus!"

"Why should I have to explain that we're a totally normal mother?!"

When Masato ad-libbed their intro, the suspicious individual twitched, and the two people inside desperately tried to correct him.

At any rate, it didn't seem like they were planning on pulling anything right this second. "Masato, move along," Shiraaase said. So he did.

"Tenth-ranked! She brought her child with her from Heaven, a veritable oracle! Seemingly drawn by the greatest of artists, an exalted angel mother! Mamariel!"

"Actually, when I put my child down for a nap, I just laze about and nibble some crackers... But I suppose I've got an image to uphold, huh?"

As divine as she was prone to speaking her mind, this mother seemed rather approachable.

"Eleventh-ranked! Described in countless stories and fables, will she give rise to yet more legends? Her blue scales glitter like jewels, the mermaid mother! Nakasao!"

"The legend of the mermaid with a child begins here! Just you wait!"

Her species was *shishamo*. An aquatic mother, appearing inside a magical sphere of water.

"Twelfth-ranked! Her favorite holiday is the Manchu Han Imperial Feast! She works as a trainer for breath attacks! The dragonewt mother! Sammo Hung!"

"Even if you aren't half dragon, you can breathe fire...once you eat my Szechuan cooking!"

Spewing out flames from her mouth with a *fwooooom* was a Chinese-style mom with dragon horns and a tail.

"Thirteenth-ranked! She survived the battles of Ragnarok with her cheery disposition intact! She's planning on skipping merrily through this fight as well! The giant mother! Kaide!"

"I'm a big momma! Everyone cheer for me! Ah-ha-haaa!"

With a body her size, a single skip caused the earth to shake. She certainly was immense.

That left only three. The end was in sight!

"Fourteenth-ranked! At a glance, she might look weak...but not once she disrobes! A human mother who has mastered matriarchal martial arts! Katou!"

"H-hi, um... F-for my children, I'll...do my best!"

A martial arts mother who seemed ordinary until you saw the muscles bulging beneath her robes.

Two more!

"Fifteenth-ranked! Hailing from a bloodline with pedigree, the first thing you see will be her gleaming fangs emerging from a shadow—a vampire mother! Kangoshii!"

"Good health begins with your teeth! When I win, brushing your teeth will become a new world rule!"

This vampire mother dressed in a nurse's uniform didn't drink blood very much—it stains your teeth.

Last one!

The final contestant strolled slowly onto the stage.

Clad in a black dress, the final mother wore a dark expression.

Oh... Her.

The woman who had straightened his hair outside the bathroom. Her intro...

"Sixteenth-ranked! Our final dark horse candidate! Everything about her, history included, is shrouded in a veil of mystery! The human mother! Hahako!"

"......"

The woman who looked so much like Mamako just stared up at Masato with hollow eyes.

At any rate, that was everyone.

These sixteen mothers would fight in a tournament to determine the world's best mother.

The crowd erupted in a round of applause for the mothers onstage. Every mother looked confident, waving back. The crowd went wild.

Meanwhile, Masato had switched off his mic and collapsed on the table.

"Nothing about that was easy... I'm so tired..."

"Tired you may be, but I have more work for you. A power only you have... Can you use that mother appraisal skill and verify that all contestants are mothers?"

"See if they truly qualify? If I'm the only one capable of doing that, then sure, I'll do it, but... Oh, right. About that. Sorente's already ruled out. That's just Amante and Sorella."

"I noticed. They each have such distinctive speech patterns."

"Right? But in the interests of safety, I assume we're just keeping tabs on them for now, yes? Anyway, I'll check the others."

Masato looked down at the mothers onstage. "Oh, Ma-kun's looking at us! Mommy's right here!" The moment he did, one of them started yelling and jumping, but he ignored her.

The one sad skill I've learned... A Child's Sense... Activate!

Masato's eyes were imbued with power, a vivid change sweeping across his vision.

The stage was bathed in carnation-red light. With this many high-level mothers together, each was giving off a vast quantity of light...

Wait, not all of them.

First, the masked, robed Sorente. There was something odd about their color.

Like they're reflecting the light around them... Is that silver robe reflective?

Or was this Amante's reflection skill? Either way, he'd already ruled them out.

But there was one other.

Oh... Hahako isn't glowing, either.

The mysterious mother who looked so uncannily like Mamako was giving off no light at all. Which meant...

While Masato pondered this, Shiraaase asked, "Well, Masato?"

"Um... I'm not seeing any reaction from Hahako at all."

"I see... Hmm..."

If she wasn't responding to Masato's skill, that meant she wasn't a mother.

If she didn't meet the conditions for entry, she should be disqualified…

"With Hahako, it doesn't matter if she responds or not. We'll allow her to participate as is."

"Huh? …You're sure?"

"This is a good opportunity to learn more about her. These matches will allow us to investigate further."

"Investigate what?"

"When it reaches a stage where I can infooorm you, I will infooorm you… Be patient for now. If you do a good job, I'll buy you some sweets later."

"Yaaay! I'll be a good boy! …Yeah, as if! Quit making fun of me!"

"Now then, if the others are all without problem, we can assume participant evaluation is complete. Do you agree?"

"Everyone else is responding normally. They're clear."

"Understood. Thank you."

Masato had certainly hoped she'd explain more.

But Shiraaase turned her mic back on and began speaking into it.

"Then we will begin drawing odds to determine the order of battles. We've prepared a tournament bracket and a draw box… If the staff in the kid's area could be so kind?"

She was, of course, addressing the three girls babysitting the children. "Don't we have enough on our plates already?" "This is a sweatshop!" "I-I'll do my best!" They were busy racing around the stage, trying to catch children scattering every which way, but now they had even more work.

Wise held the box, seemingly past the point of caring about the children climbing up her legs and back.

Medhi was equally swarmed but managed to check the balls the mothers drew anyway.

Porta got the giant child to hold her up so she could write the mothers' names on the tournament bracket.

The fruits of their labor completed the bracket. The first round would be as follows:

*   *   *

Match 1: The Hero's Mother Mamako vs Beastkin Mother Growlette
Match 2: Mermaid Mother Nakasao vs Devil Mother Invi
Match 3: Martial Artist Mother Katou vs Android Mother Mechatte
Match 4: Dragonewt Mother Sammo Hung vs Elf Mother Chaliele
Match 5: Suspicious Mother Sorente vs Vampire Mother Kangoshii
Match 6: Fairy Mother Nympha vs Giant Mother Kaide
Match 7: Mysterious Mother Hahako vs Spirit Mother Etheria
Match 8: Angel Mother Mamariel vs Ninja Mother Kunoichiko

The contestants went back to the waiting rooms to get ready. Since the actual contents of the matches would be decided directly beforehand, they had to prepare for anything—meaning they'd need cooking implements, cleaning apparatuses, laundry supplies, and even weapons.

As the other mothers hastily ran around, Mamako got ready.

"Well, I certainly need my battle apron. I'd better equip that special apron Ma-kun gave me! Hee-hee!"

Equipping the apron Masato had acquired from the school gacha over her usual gear, she was ready. She waited excitedly for her turn.

Staring fixedly at Mamako...was the suspicious mother, Sorente.

Four eyes staring from a safe distance away.

"It's almost the main affaaaair. I'm really feeling the pressuuuure."

"Yeah. But we've already overcome the toughest hurdles. When the contestants were introduced, Masato Oosuki must have used that skill of his that identifies mothers. But we anticipated that. Since we knew he used the light they give off to identify them, we made this masked robe of reflective materials..."

"You don't need to explain this to meeee. More importantly, start waaalking."

"I—I know! I'm curious if that other special being is lurking among these mothers, but...first, we'd better handle Mamako Oosuki."

The suspicious mother, Sorente, began to move.

Apparently, Amante couldn't see very well. "Oh, sorryyyy." "......" They'd nearly bumped into the mysterious mother, Hahako.

But Sorente suspiciously made their way over to Mamako.

"Um... Do you have a miiinute?"

"Oh, what is it? You're—?"

"Sorenteeee. We've never met befooore. Don't worryyy. We're a totally normal mooother."

"Oh, really? Your voice sounds so familiar... But I guess not."

"N-n-not at aaaall! Just a coiiiincidence! Seriously, think nothing of iiiit. Anywaaay..."

Sorente's body thrashed suspiciously, and then they pulled out a small bottle containing a reddish-brown liquid.

"This is a gift for you, Maaamako. Someone shared one of those treats you were haaanding out. So I thought I'd thank yooou. Drink this right awaaay!"

"Oh, you shouldn't have! And I was just thinking how thirsty I was! I'd be delighted to accept."

Mamako seemed to suspect nothing. She took the bottle and immediately downed it.

In that moment, both girls under the masked robe pumped their fists in secret. "Well thennn, enjoy your maaatch!" And with that, Sorente departed, suspiciously fast.

And once they were far enough away, they pumped fists again.

"Mwa-ha-haaa! That was so eeeeasy!"

"Apparently... Didn't expect her to just chug it like that..."

"I think her mind was entirely on the present from Masatooo. Stiiiill... it doesn't maaatter. As long as she drank it, she's doooooomed."

"Heh, exactly... That's a slow-acting poison. Now that she's downed it, it'll slowly whittle away her strength..."

"And when she's weakened, the two of us will attack togeeether! Mwa-ha-haaa!"

"Just to be absolutely clear, we aren't afraid of Mamako Oosuki. I could definitely best her in a normal fight. But fighting her in top form would be quite a challenge, and rather than be reckless, I'd prefer to fight her in a condition where we're guaranteed to win..."

"No need to explain the obvious truuuth. Geez, Amante, just shut uuup..."

Two of the infamous Four Heavenly Kings had certainly turned into massive cowards.

With everyone ready, it was time to begin.

"Now then, Masato. Almost time," urged Shiraaase.

"You're going to insist the two of us keep doing commentary, huh?"

He would definitely have preferred to resign.

Masato looked down at the kid's area around the stage and saw Wise about to blow her top, Medhi's eyes gone dead, and Porta looking sadder than ever before—all three staring wordlessly up at him.

If they were risking their lives babysitting, it was hardly fair for him to escape alone. Doing so would put his party's bonds and Masato's own life in danger.

"Well, Masato, now that you understand the predicament you're in, let's begin."

"Right! I'm just thrilled to do play-by-plays or commentary! Love to work! …Thanks for waiting, everyone! The first match is about to begin!"

Staring at the script through his tears, Masato began talking. The crowd roared.

The first match contestants—Mamako and the beastkin mother, Growlette—stepped onto the stage.

"Growlette, I'm really looking forward to this." Mamako smiled.

"It's finally time! Mamako, you'd better be ready!" Growlette growled.

Both seemed fired up. This battle would be a fierce one.

It was time to decide the contents of their match.

"Erm… Looks like you have your hands full with those children, so sorry, but… Wise, can you get the match draw box?"

"Sure, sure! Whatever! Argh, you'll pay for this, Masato!"

"Why are you mad at me?! None of this was my idea!"

Just like with the brackets, Wise held the box, ignoring the children around her. "Go on, Mamako!"

"Why, thank you." Since her prelim rank was higher, it was Mamako's right to draw.

And the ball she pulled out read…

*   *   *

CLEANING (DANGER LEVEL: MAX)

The first match would be a super-dangerous cleaning contest.

"Uh, so we're starting right off with a doozy, I guess… Shiraaase, what exactly does this mean?"

"This battle will involve cleaning the area we've prepared while searching for an important item and simultaneously avoiding anything dangerous. Eyes to the stage, please!"

Masato and the crowd turned to look.

Magic circles appeared on the wooden floors of the stage…summoning desks, chairs, beds, bookshelves, and other furniture.

Everything summoned was evenly distributed—half around Mamako and half around Growlette.

"I see. Just like cleaning a real bedroom…but all this furniture appears to be clean already."

"From a distance, perhaps it does. However…"

The eyes of the mothers onstage were clearly locking onto a number of areas in need of attention.

"There's definitely dust in the gaps between those bookshelves… Oh my!" exclaimed Mamako. "And under the bed, way at the very back. The underside, too!"

"The kinds of places you might overlook even if you think you've cleaned properly!" said Growlette. "They definitely want to remind us to be thorough! That's what I call a challenge!"

"Hee-hee, yes. Definitely a chance to show Mommy's skills."

Mamako and Growlette were certainly feeling competitive. They were tightening their apron strings, snapping fingers, engines revved and ready to rumble.

Then Masato noticed something.

"Huh? That's weird… The layout of that furniture looks familiar…"

"Additionally, the rooms prepared onstage re-create the actual real-world layout of the bedroom of the hero accompanying his mother on this adventure."

"…Huh?"

"Today they will be cleaning a child's bedroom. While they clean, they will be tasked with retrieving items that should have been shown to parents, yet got lost—while also avoiding contact with things parents are better off not seeing. A real test of a parent's discretion. Additionally, these hidden items are also reproducing the real-world bedroom."

"Huh? What? Why? Stop, stop; back up! Waaaaait!"

"No waiting! Ready... MOM IT!"

With Shiraaase's signal, the battle began.

The beastkin mother, Growlette, was the first to jump into action. She started with cleaning.

"Got any hard-to-clean nooks and crannies? Ha-ha! For a beastkin, that's child's play! After all...I have this!"

Facing one such nook, Growlette turned around...

...and stuck her fluffy tail in it!

It rummaged all around inside before she pulled it out.

"Ha-ha! Well? Quite a score!"

The gap was certainly polished clean! But her tail was now filthy...

This was a special beastkin mom skill, one that used the beastkin body to the fullest—A Cleaning Tail!

No, hang on.

"Heeeeey! What theeeeee—?!"

Masato found himself leaning out of the broadcast booth, loudly protesting. How could he possibly let this go unchallenged?

"What's wrong, Masato? What's gotten into you?" asked Shiraaase.

"What's wrong?! That's all wrong! She's got a beautiful fluffy tail! And we're just going to let her clean with it?! That's completely unacceptable!"

"It is?"

"Yes! ...Listen! Tails are a luxury item! Something to stare at longingly, touch gently, appreciating the soft caress against your cheek as you reach sky-high bliss! They must be respected!"

"If something's useful, you oughta use it! It ain't goin' anywhere!"

It was her property, and she had every right to reject any criticism. Besides, it WAS attached to her.

"Augh! Aughhhhh! This is why mothers are—!"

Masato slapped the desk repeatedly, making a show of his torment, but Growlette just laughed him off. "You sure are a lively one! Ah-ha-ha!"

Clearly, she was well versed in dealing with children's temper tantrums.

Growlette continued sticking her tail behind the clock, under the bed, and all around. Getting her hands…well, tail, dirty as she tidied up.

"It easily cleans even the fussiest spots! Tails can be moved at will! …Well, Mamako? Can you beat my tail cleaning? Oh, I forgot! You don't have a tail! Bwa-ha-ha-ha!"

Certain of victory, she began to boast.

Meanwhile…

"O-oh? …What's going on…? I'm feeling a bit funny…"

…Mamako wasn't moving at all. Her hand was on her stomach, and she'd gone very pale.

Sorente was watching from the shadows of the entrance hall, grinning. But no one noticed that. Their eyes were elsewhere.

Growlette, Masato, Shiraaase, the babysitting staff, the audience—everyone was staring at one thing only.

"…Unh… Oooh…"

Mamako had collapsed to her knees. In agony.

The moment she did, Masato vaulted over the broadcast table.

"H-hey! Mom?! Mom! What's wrong?"

"I-I'm fine… Mommy's fine. Don't worry about—"

"No, you're not fine! You're clearly unwell!"

He didn't know what to do. His mind went blank. He ran to her side, ready to burst into tears, frantically calling her name…

…and then a pair of triangular ears, covered in red-and-blue fur, appeared on Mamako's head.

And then two tails, one with red fur and one with blue, stretched out from her back.

"…Uh?"

She'd just sprouted animal ears.

Mamako, now adorned with animal ears and two tails, got back to her feet.

"Oh? I feel much better all of a sudden! I wonder what that was? …Well, no time to waste! I'm in the middle of a contest! I'd better get to work!"

"No, um, Mom…?"

"Ma-kun, just you watch! Mommy's gonna work her hardest! …Now, if I'm going to clean, I'll need… Oh? Look what I found! These tails would be perfect!"

Animal Mamako immediately spied the practical applications of her tails and began cleaning with them.

On her right: the tail resembling the Holy Sword of Mother Earth.

On her left: the tail resembling the Holy Sword of Mother Ocean.

"All right! ...*Hyah!*"

The red tail thrust into a gap between the furniture, and when she pulled it out...all the dust was gone! Fresh as a daisy!

At the same time, the blue tail made a sideways sweep under the bed, cleaning all the dirt!

Animal Mamako didn't stop her tidying there. "I see more dust! And more there!" Tiny gaps, narrow crannies, openings beneath, detailed woodwork—her tails cleaned it all.

"Well, the cleaning's all done! Now I just have to check everything over..."

Even her cleaning was two-hit and multi-target!

Mamako's cleaning area was flawlessly polished!

"There you go! Hee-hee!"

"Argh... Even my mom's using her tails to clean..."

"I—I never...," stammered Growlette. "Cleaning with two tails... I could never do that, no matter how hard I tried... But I'm not done yet! This contest is about more than cleaning!"

That's right. Cleaning was merely the prelude. The key to victory was to avoid the dangerous items in the children's rooms and recover the critical ones. Growlette changed tactics, moving with beastly speeds.

This was met with passionate cheers.

"Under the bed! I'm sure of it! There's gotta be something!"

"Check the shelves! They might be disguised as normal books!"

"They aren't! I've got nothing! You two shut up!"

Masato jumped down to the kid's area to silence Wise and Medhi, but he was too late.

Growlette was staring at the corner of the carpet, deep in thought.

"Hmm... That section isn't lying flat... There's something under there! ...But it's not thick enough to be a magazine... In which case, it's mine!"

"Augh! That's—!"

The thin book pulled from underneath the carpet was…

…a plastic card with a beautiful anime girl on it! If you tilted the card right, her clothes would vanish, leaving her without a stitch on! Scandalous!

This was an item parents were better off not knowing about! A failure!

"My goodness…," said Growlette. "Not only do I have to pretend I never saw this, it carries with it the danger that my child is only interested in 2-D girls…!"

"No, that's not true… I promise… I didn't even buy that myself—it came with an issue of *Dragon* magazine… Trust me… Please… You gotta believe me…"

Growlette hung her head. Still, she couldn't help but marvel, "It's truly just like the real thing…!" Masato was seriously on the verge of death.

But he could not afford to die here. Animal Mamako was on the prowl.

"Ma-kun, don't worry. Mommy knows better than to touch the encyclopedia on those shelves."

"Oh! That would be a great help— Uh… No, wait!"

"Everything will be just fine! Mommy's eyes know how to find only what Mommy should be seeing!"

"No, no, no, what are you doing?!"

Animal Mamako's eyes focused, searching the restaged room.

He desperately wanted her to stop, but…Mamako had something perhaps all parents have: the special child's room search skill, A Mother's Search!

After a long, careful look around—"Oh! Right there!"—Animal Mamako dashed over to the desk, pulled open a drawer, and felt around inside.

And she pulled out…a letter from his school, advising parents of an upcoming parent's day.

This was something a parent was supposed to see, so she was right to find it!

"Oh my! Ma-kun, did you think I didn't want to go? If it's for you, I'd happily come to parent's day!"

"That's why I didn't want you to see it! You always get there first! And whenever you go to school for stuff like this, the other kids and teachers all act like a movie star showed up! I hate it!"

Masato clearly had his reasons for keeping it hidden, but…

…the match was decided.

"Dual tail cleaning, flawless search procedures… You're incredible. It's frustrating, but I've clearly lost!" Growlette hung her head, admitting defeat.

"This match's victory goes to Mamako!" Shiraaase announced. "Congratulations."

A fanfare echoed, and the crowd gave her a standing ovation. They applauded not just Animal Mamako's victory, but Growlette's gracious concession.

"Growlette, thank you."

"I'm glad I got a chance to fight you. Thanks!"

The two mothers shook hands. Such a beautiful sight!

But there was one boy who couldn't let it end that easily.

"I've had about enough… The way you treat tails was one thing, but what about how you treat me?!"

Masato was ready to unleash the full force of his fury, but before he could…

"Ughhhh?! Wh-wh-wh-what giiives?! We poisoned herrr! How could it end like thiiis?!"

"Huh?! Oh, that's right—Mamako Oosuki's equipment gives her flawless defense against status effects… But why did she conveniently grow ears and a tail…?"

"Ohhhh! That's riiight! She has that super-cheaty skiiiill! It makes everything work out her waaay!"

"She does?! Is that what happened?!"

Masato's rant was drowned out by an argument that so helpfully explained what had just occurred.

"Dang! Retreat!" "Auuuuughh…?!"

When he turned, there was no one there.

The first match of round one was complete.

The furniture summoned for the cleaning battle was quickly removed…or should have been.

But an innocent force had claimed the stage.

"Picture books!" "Missy, read dis!" "Read it!" "Hurry!" "Read to us!"

"This isn't the time to read picture books! You've got to get off the stage! Please listen to us! We're begging you!" Pestered by five beastkin children, Wise was on the verge of tears.

"Whoooa! I'm…flyyy…iiiing…"

"Ohhh?! A gust of wind caught the fairy child, and…!"

"Bed! So big! Yay! Yaaaa……" *Zzzzzzzz…*

"Eeeeek! That's bad! If the mermaid child sleeps on the bed, it'll absorb all her water, and she'll dry out!!"

Medhi was dealing with two crises at once.

"Let's play dolly!"

"Er, um… Am I the doll?"

The giant child picked up Porta and sat her on a chair. Porta was clearly at a complete loss.

The children's onslaught showed no signs of abating. The stage was more of a war zone than it had been during the actual match.

But while the babysitters were in trouble, the audience was eating it up. "Hang in there, girls!" "Don't let them win!" The audience was cheering on their babysitting efforts, a smile on every face.

This was a brilliant way to keep the crowd entertained between matches. "I haaate this!" "Someone help me! Heeeelp!" "I—I think I'm gonna cry…," shouted Wise, Medhi, and Porta, in turn. A beautiful display.

Anyway.

In the broadcast booth were Shiraaase, Mamako (her ears and tail long gone), Masato, and the beastkin mother, Growlette. It was time for an interview.

"The two of you had a wonderful match! We'd like to hear more… First, Mamako, you pulled off an incredible victory, but what do you think led to it?"

"Well, naturally, Ma-kun's support! Ma-kun really thinks about how Mommy feels and gives me such strength! Hee-hee!"

"I don't actually have any buff skills. Nor did I actually do much of anything…"

"That's not true!" Growlette declared. "When Mamako started looking unwell, you came running! You're a good boy who cares deeply for his mother!"

She slapped him hard on the back. "Uh, that hurt..." "Don't worry about it! Ah-ha-ha!" A boisterous mother not about to let Masato's slowly draining HP gauge bother her. Enthusiasm was dangerous.

"We all know a mother's strength comes from her kids," she said. "I guess that *was* what decided the match... Oh, but if Masato becomes my son, the next match would be mine! Right, let's do that! Masato, be my kid!"

"Wha—? Where'd that come from?"

"Good idea, yeah? Oh, I know! Masato, you like tails, right? Well, go ahead!"

Growlette began waving her tail in front of his face. She'd groomed it after the match, so there was no dust or grime left—it was a lovely, fluffy tail once more.

"You touch a young beastkin's tail, and they'll be all 'Eek!' or 'You pervert!' but I'm already a mom! I can handle a little touchy-feely. Go on and fluff that tail all you like."

"Er... Seriously?"

"Totally! I mean it! Go on, help yourself!"

Masato found the tail's fluff very tempting. It was calling to him: *Come on. Go ahead. Fluff me.* The ultimate sensation, right in front of him.

Uh-oh... I dunno if I can resist...

Masato's hand reached forward of its own accord, ready to savor the bliss...

...but someone behind him tugged his sleeve, and he snapped out of it.

When he turned around—

"Now, Ma-kun! You're making Mommy hopping mad!"

—Mamako's cheeks were all puffed up in a major sulk. Super-jealous. Any time one of the other mothers tempted Masato, it sparked Mamako's envy.

This activated the special skill A Mother's Envy, and she started storing up energy...

...but her oblivious son failed to notice.

"Mom! Knock that off! You're way too old to sulk like that; seriously, just don't, please."

"Mommy's so mad!" she fumed.

"You're getting worse! Why?! Why is my mom always like this?!"

"You two are so close! I'm so jealous… Now I want Masato even more!" said Growlette.

"My, my," remarked Shiraaase. "Masato's in demand!"

"Yeesh! This is, like, the one situation where that's not a positive thing!"

"And with that, our interview concludes. The first match is over, with Mamako as the victor! You'll see her again in the first match of round two tomorrow! Don't miss it!"

"Augh, Shiraaase! Don't just wrap things up. Do something about these mothers!"

"Do something about these kids first! Seriously!"

"Help us! We'll do anything! Wise will do anything!"

"E-er… I'm scared she's going to start changing my clothes soon…"

While Masato was trapped between his real mother and someone else's…

…the girls onstage were trapped in the furious—nay, deadly battle called babysitting.

As these battles continued with no end in sight, the first day drew to a close.

Mamako had claimed victory in the first round and advanced to the second.

The remaining match results were as follows:

Match 2: Mermaid Mother Nakasao (Loser) vs Devil Mother Invi (Winner)

A shopping battle. Nakasao, being a mermaid, used her Appraise skill at the fishmonger to score a big advantage, but the succubus's allure overwhelmed the staff, who gave Invi a huge discount and the victory.

"The legend of the mermaid with a child ends here…"

"No one can resist the allure of a devil mama. Hahhh."

Match 3: Martial Arts Mother Katou (L) vs Android Mother Mechatte (W)

A sewing battle. Katou used her well-honed muscles to sew stiff denim bare-handed, but the android mother converted her flying drones into a lightning-fast sewing machine and claimed victory.

"My muscles weep... But I gave it my best shot and accept the results."

"Your matriarchal energy is off the charts. With respect, I've added you to my group of mom friends. Let us compete again someday."

Match 4: Dragonewt Mother Sammo Hung (L) vs Elf Mother Chaliele (W)

"What? Dragonewt children love spicy food! These results make no sense!"

"The bounty of the forest is loved by all races. Elves are proud to live in harmony with the woods."

A cooking battle. Sammo Hung had gone with her specialty, ultra-spicy Szechuan cuisine. The flavor was definitely top class.

But it proved too spicy for normal children to eat, and Chaliele claimed victory with a dish made from mushrooms harvested on the spot.

Match 5: Suspicious Mother Sorente (W) vs Vampire Mother Kangoshii (L)

A cleaning battle. The vampire mother seemed confident in her cleaning skills but inexplicably was unable to perform at her usual level.

"I'm a vampire, yet I couldn't quite sink my teeth in... How can this be?"

"Oh myyyy? Is that aaaaall you've got? Another lousy moooom! Mwa-ha-haaa!"

Belittling their opponent, Sorente languidly swept the match.

Match 6: Fairy Mother Nympha (L) vs Giant Mother Kaide (W)

"La-la-la-laaa! Ah-ha-ha! I won somehow! Yay!"

A dog-walking battle. The difference in size was what clinched it; Kaide was able to cover the distance the dog wanted, merrily skipping all the way.

As for the fairy mother...

"Oh, do excuse me. The winds are calling—I'm not fleeing the scene of my defeat or anything, just so you know."

Nympha had been blown away by the winds generated by her opponent's skipping and never returned.

She was still MIA.

Match 7: Mysterious Mother Hahako (W) vs Spirit Mother Etheria (L)

"………"

"We were actually four against one—and still…" "How'd we lose?" "Luck of the draw." "Clearly…"

A PTA-meeting battle. PTA meetings involved doling out duties that could be a lot of work. But since Etheria was actually four different spirits fused together, four such jobs were pressed upon her, and she was forced to give up.

The mysterious mother simply stood there looking gloomy—everyone was afraid to talk to her, and she was avoided completely.

Match 8: Angel Mother Mamariel (L) vs Ninja Mother Kunoichiko (W)

A battle over dropping off and picking up children. Mamariel soared through the air, kids in tow, easily clearing the first checkpoint. But the sight of her divine visage drew a crowd, stopping her in her tracks and preventing her from continuing.

Kunoichiko made it through all the checkpoints with a flawless ninja run.

"I may have lost, but all is well. I shall return home and play halo toss with my children."

"I'm a mom and a ninja! The ultimate combo! …Oh, gotta be sneaky…"

Since everyone entered in the World Matriarchal Arts Tournament was a mother, the first day ended, as planned, at three o'clock, giving them time to take in the laundry and shop for dinner.

ANIMAL
MAMAKO

SKILLS

STATS

A CLEANING TAIL
If she finds dirt or dust, her tail can wipe it down. Very useful.

A CHILD-MINDING TAIL
If her hands are full, she can cuddle demanding children with her tail.

STRENGTHS

Her tail is super useful for cleaning and child care. Even Masato can't keep his eyes off the fluff!

WEAKNESSES

Her hearty, carnivorous disposition leads to her mostly cooking whole roasts on the bone and other rugged dishes. Her physical abilities are off the charts, so when washing clothes by hand, she can easily damage the fabric.

STATS

MATERNITY: 100 / COOKING: 70 / LAUNDRY: 70
CLEANING: 100 / SHOPPING: 90 / COMBAT: 120
MA-KUN: 100

SPECIAL   FLUFFINESS: 100

Chapter 3 The Staff Fight Harder than the Contestants and Take More Damage. Why?

Clear skies for the second day of the World Matriarchal Arts Tournament.

The inn's garden was bathed in sunlight, even this early. A perfect day for laundry.

"Let's get these hung out to dry! ...Masato, can you step back a bit?"

"Uh, sure."

Chaliele scattered some tiny seeds on the ground. They quickly sprouted, stalks rising.

They grew into tall, thin trees with branches shaped like hangers.

"Wow... Those are bizarre-looking. What are they?"

"Trees for hanging laundry! Your first time seeing them?"

"Completely. You even grow your own laundry lines... Elf moms are amazing. But, uh... Wait, are they moving?"

"Yes, these trees move. The elves live deep in the forest, and not much sunlight makes it through the leaves. So as you can see..."

Masato's shirt and a pair of underwear belonging to—he wasn't sure, but definitely a girl—were hung on the tree.

The clothes-hanger tree tiptoed around on its roots before finding a good, sunny spot. "See? Isn't that handy?" "Definitely." He meant it. Every home should have one.

But he couldn't stand around being impressed all day.

"Masato! Over here! Gimme a hand!"

"Uh, sure! Got it!"

The mother calling him was the beastkin, Growlette. She was lugging some rolled-up futons. "Where do we hang that...?" "Here's fine! Hah!" Growlette slammed her fist into the ground. It cracked, and a rock slab shot up out of it.

"Let's get these futons aired out! It's a beautiful day, perfect for the task!"

"R-right... So beastkin moms use underground rock slabs to hang futons... Incredible stuff..."

"Oh, have you seen Nympha around? Since we're doing laundry anyway, I'd love it if she could give me a hand..."

"You called?" the fairy said, popping out.

"Augh! You were in my pocket again?!"

Nympha poked her head out of Masato's shirt pocket, then flew upward on butterfly wings.

She burrowed into the laundry, rubbing against it, then rolled across the futons. "...What are you doing?" "Take a whiff, and you'll see." Masato sniffed the clothing she'd rubbed against.

"Whoa! That smells amazing! Like really good fabric softener!"

"If you have a fairy mother around, your clothes and rooms will all smell like flowers. No need for air fresheners!"

"Everyday elegance! Fairy mothers are awesome!"

"Thank you. Even if it's just flattery, having my son say that makes me happy."

"No, no, it's not flattery at— Wait, did you just make me your son?"

Her work done, Nympha settled on Masato's head for a rest. "Uh... About that son thing..." She just started blowing bubbles, striking an elegant pose.

Either way, the task was done.

One son and three moms stood together, watching the laundry flutter in the breeze.

"Uh, so thanks for your help, Moms."

"Thank you, Masato. Your help made the work go by that much faster."

"No, no... I barely helped at all... I spent the whole time being amazed by the skills of mothers of other races."

"Quit being so modest! Getting up early to help us moms out is a good thing! You're a good boy!"

"Not everyone would do that. You really are a wonderful son, Masato."

"Th-thanks... Actually, there was a different reason for that, but, uh... Ha-ha."

The reason why he'd woken up early to help out was...

*　　*　　*

Meanwhile, inside the inn.

All hell was breaking loose.

"Arghhh! Please! Just put something on! Get dressed!"

"No!" "No clothes!" "Missy's got pink undies!"

"Because you're all running around, and we're supposed to be watching you, we can't get dressed either! So please start by putting on some clothes!"

"You've got white undies!" "Undies!" "Und— Erk…!"

"Eep! The mermaid child is drying out! I'll carry her to the sink and get her wet!"

"Porta's undies have a bunny!" "Cute!" "Cute!"

First thing that morning, Growlette had barged in and hauled all the laundry away. The result: The beastkin children, the mermaid child, and the fairy child were all running naked through the halls.

Like the kids, Growlette had pulled the girls' pajamas off, leaving them in their underwear, but before they had a chance to get dressed, they'd been swarmed.

That was hardly a place Masato could afford to hang around. Ever.

Seeing girls in their undies was wrong…and that gentlemanly reason might even be a small part of it.

More than anything else, though, he simply didn't want to be involved. He'd made an emergency escape, picked the garden at random, and encountered the mothers dealing with the laundry. That was the only reason he was here.

But that was a secret.

Back to the laundry area of the garden…

Masato was talking to the other mothers again.

"But I was pretty surprised last night, Growlette. You just showed up out of nowhere and announced you'd be staying here now!"

"Turn a blind eye to that, please. We lost our battles, so they kicked us out of our inns…but just heading back home with my tail between my legs ain't happening, got it?"

"I, at least, wanted to see the rest of the tournament. So I was searching for other lodgings when I happened to run into this committee member named Shiraaase…"

"Oh, okay. She hooked you up, huh? Nothing she can't do."

"I believe there are several others staying here as well… See, over there!"

Chaliele pointed at a corner of the inn.

A familiar-looking middle-aged woman was standing there, holding a watering can.

"Oh…? Isn't that…the martial artist? Katou, was it?"

"Y-yes! That's right! Good morning!"

When Masato called out, she came hustling over with a watering can in hand.

"M-Masato! Would you train with me?"

"Er… Train? With a watering can?"

"Yes! The martial arts taught in my home begin by honing your body through household chores…and I'm sure they'll make you stronger, Masato! Try it!"

"Me? Stronger?! I'm in! Please tell me more!"

Hooked by his favorite phrase, Masato started training with her.

Standing by the flower beds, legs spread shoulder width apart, hips lowered, arms outstretched, holding a full watering can steady, slowly tipping it…

"Oof… This definitely takes its toll on your arms and legs… But I can handle it…"

"Well done. Your muscles are in top form."

"You mean it? Actually, I've been thinking the same thing lately, you know."

"You have the raw talent, Masato… If only you could marry my daughter, become my son, and inherit the dojo… I'm starting to seriously consider the possibility."

"I've got that much talent? Wow! Ah-ha-ha!"

Just as he was beginning to ponder becoming a martial artist…

"Back up!"

…Growlette and the other mothers, who'd been watching with smiles, suddenly surrounded Masato, glaring at him.

"We're not about to let that pass!"

"Yeah! You aren't the only one trying to make Masato your son, Katou!"

"Were you not aware that he is already *my* son?"

"Er, um… What?"

It was like someone had hit a gong, signifying the start of a war over Masato.

"You want a mom with pointy elf ears, right?" *Twitch, twitch.*

"Look, Masato! A tail! You love tails!" *Fluff, fluff.*

"Masato—I'm a handy portable mom you can have with you all the time." *Rub, rub.*

"P-please be the child of this super-ripped mom!" *Flex, flex.*

"What? What's going on? Being surrounded by women is supposed to be a good thing, but they're all moms—what even is this?!"

A mom with legendary ears. A mom with a fluffy tail. A mom you can keep in your pocket. A mom who could bench press with the best of them. Each putting their greatest sales pitch forward, tempting him, trying to get him to be their son. It was… It was…

…not something Mother Earth would let stand.

"Mm? Is the ground shaking? This slight trembling underfoot— No?!"

A special mom skill that pinpointed her son's location and forcibly disrupted whatever was happening there.

A Mother's Fangs.

An instant later, the ground between Masato and the mothers erupted. "Augh?!" A massive earth spike forced its way up between them. This was, of course, the work of…

"Oh, Ma-kun! There you are! Mommy's on her way!"

As Masato fell to the ground, Mamako came running full speed in his direction, Terra di Madre in one hand. Yep. She'd done it again. This was all her fault.

"Hey, Mom! What the hell? You can't go scaring people like—!"

"So this is the fabled motherly fretting skill." *Nod, nod.*

"She is a mother. She's bound to fret." *Nod, nod.*

"Very handy when you don't want your son stolen." *Nod, nod.*

"And her instincts tell her when it's needed." *Nod, nod.*

They all seemed to take it in stride. Like it was normal.

Meanwhile...

"Wh-what the—?! What happened?!"

"This is...Mamako's skill, A Mother's Fangs!"

"Wow, that surprised me!"

Three girls in their underwear were leaning out the window. "Geez! Don't scare us!" "It wasn't my fau—mmph?!" A pillow smacked Masato in the face. Cruelty!

But Mamako was here now.

"Ma-kun, good morning! It's your mommy!"

"Yeah, yeah, no need to remind me. I know who you are. You aren't an elf or a beastkin or a fairy or insanely buff... Other than your unnaturally youthful looks, you're a perfectly normal mom."

"Okay! If you want me to be, I'll become a special mommy! An elf or a beastkin or a fairy or muscle-bound or whatever you want! Just you watch!"

"Huh?"

Mamako had clenched her fist, straining herself. "Hnggggg... *Hyah!*" Then she released it—and voilà!

Mamako remained unchanged.

"Hmm? That's odd... I thought if I just thought about Ma-kun, I could become anything... Now Mommy's sad."

"I'm actually super-relieved we've found a limit to how ridiculously OP you can be...," said Masato.

"Oh my! You don't seem to be your usual self, Mamako... I hate to see you like this. This is a time to send salt to your enemy."

This expression did not mean literally giving spices as gifts. It meant to assist your enemy in a predicament rather than take advantage of their misfortune.

Chaliele pulled a small bottle filled with grass-green liquid out of her clothing.

"Here—perfectly ordinary green tea," she said, grinning.

"I see. That means it definitely isn't," replied Masato.

"Eh-heh-heh. Sorry... This is a secret elf potion. If she drinks it, she'll be transformed into an elf. It's perfectly safe and can be found anywhere in the world. It's made by the settlement's tourism board."

"...Tourism board...?"

"Elf settlements are suffering from population declines... The young elves all want to leave home. We're always shorthanded. We've been forced to take these drastic measures to shore up the number of residents..."

"It's a tough world, and I don't want to hear about it. Let's get back to fantasy, please?"

"Ah, y-yes. No need for such depressing thoughts. So, Mamako... would you like to be an elf?"

"Of course! I'd love to be one if that would make Ma-kun happy!"

Mamako immediately chugged the elf potion.

A flash of green light enveloped her, and her ears stretched out, her hair turned gold...

Mamako became an elf!

"Wow! You're really an elf, Mom!"

"Oh my! My! ...Ma-kun, how is it? Do you like Mommy now?"

"Well, uh..."

Blond hair. Definitely pointy on the ear front. The holy ears of the fantasy race Masato loved the most!

Elf Mamako was shoving her ears at him!

"Hmm... But basically, you're still my real mom, so...it doesn't really do it for me."

"Oh no!" *Shock!*

Your mom is still your mom. Nothing could change that. Nothing at all.

With the morning's commotion over, the group headed for the tournament hall.

Like the day before, the street was teeming with audience members. People of all races were lined up, excited for the day's battles.

Many eyes turned toward Masato's group, but...well, can you blame them?

After all, they were quite a spectacle. Mamako was the star of the tournament, and behind her was the elf, Chaliele, who had also advanced to the second round, and the beastkin, Growlette, who Mamako had defeated the day before—three very famous mothers.

Masato himself seemed to be getting a fair amount of attention.

There was a glittering halo floating above his head and white wings on his back. His right hand was imbued with the power of fire, his left hand with water, and his feet with earth and wind.

Every part of him was illuminated; the overall effect was so gaudy he wanted to cry.

"An angel's halo and wings definitely suit the chosen hero of the sky."

"We've given him the spirits' power!" "This'll be great!" "Definitely." "Masato's a hero!"

"I'm utterly flattered, really… But right now I really wish you wouldn't."

"This is an honor you deserve! The hero has a right to the angel's power! …Perhaps I'll take you back to my home in Heaven and make you my son! Ha-ha."

"We agree." "To accept Masato." "As a child." "Of the spirits."

"That all sounds very heroic and has a nice ring to it, but still, I'd definitely prefer it if you stopped that."

They'd run into the angel mother, Mamariel, and the spirit mother, Etheria, on the way, and they'd become quite taken with him, leading to this result. "Ma-kun?! Your mommy is right here!" Mamako was instantly forcing herself on him again, and it was awful. Exhausting.

Masato was ready to just give up on everything and make a run for it, but…

…given the battles his party members were about to face, that hardly seemed fair. Everyone had a long road in front of them.

"Hey, missy, what's thaaat?" "Let's go see!" "Let's gooo!"

"I said *Don't wander off!* Hey! Hold hands! Seriously!"

"Missy, can I get a huuuug?" "Hug!" "I'm gonna ride your head! Hup!"

"Wh-why do you like us so much?! Your mothers are right here! You can totally go to them instead!!"

"I'm gonna go to Mama!" "Me too!" "Let's spirit fuse with that boy!" "Yeah!"

"Ahhh! Fighter child, angel child, spirit children! Don't go! Masato will only get in more trouble!"

Wise, Medhi, and Porta all had their hands full watching the children. Masato shot them a sympathetic glance.

This is our adventure...and we're always playing on hard mode.

An adventure with one mom was hard enough. They knew that only too well.

But add other mothers into the mix and have them be big on free-range parenting, and the adventure's difficulty rating shot skyward with no cap in sight.

It was enough to bring the waterworks, regardless of who was watching.

If this game has a god, please...we just want a normal adventure where we fight some monsters...

Masato offered a heartfelt prayer.

And as he did, they reached their destination.

Shiraaase was waiting for them at the back of the tournament hall, outside the entrance for staff and contestants.

"Oh, is everyone arriving together?"

"Yeah, and our suffering grows ever stronger. Please offer some assistance. We're really at the ends of our ropes here."

"I see. I was intending to tease you mercilessly, Masato, but I get the impression you might actually punch me if I did. Instead, why don't you all come this way?"

Shiraaase looked mildly disappointed but did her duty.

"First, Mamako, Chaliele. You both have matches, so please head inside to the waiting rooms."

"Right... Okay, Ma-kun! Mommy's going inside!"

"Yeah, yeah. I know you're my mom; stop trying to hammer that point home. And take care."

"Masato, have you nothing to say to your elf mother?"

"Good luck, Chaliele! I'll be rooting for you like I would anyone else I know."

"Oh my! Rejected. Such a shame. Hee-hee."

Subtly showing off her ears, Chaliele headed inside. Mamako tried to do the same. "It's not a competition!" She was a handful, but he finally managed to see her off.

Next up were the mothers who'd lost in the first round.

"Growlette, Nympha, Katou, Mamariel, and Etheria. We've pre-pared special seats for all the main tournament participants and their children. Please head to the stands."

"AND their kids?!"

"You're taking them with you?!"

"I'm sure I heard that! Shiraaase said so!"

The girls pounced on those words, like they were their salvation. Tears of joy welled up...but...

"Preparing seats for us is a nice gesture," Growlette said. "But my kids are still so little... I doubt they'd be able to sit still for it."

"Er...b-but...then you can look after them!"

"That's true, but...I really think I'd end up getting sucked into the fights. If only there was a place where I could let the kids do as they pleased..."

"I don't think anywhere like that exists! No, it definitely doesn't! No such thing!"

"Oh, wasn't there a kid's space around the stage?"

"Um—um! Ch-children should be with their mothers!"

The three girls fought valiantly against the gathering storm clouds. With all their might, not giving an inch!

Growlette cast them a sidelong glance...and grinned.

"Don't worry. I'm not gonna force my kids on you. It's simple! I'm just gonna watch from the kid's space."

"Yes, that way we can watch the tournament while letting our kids run free."

"Oh, that's an excellent idea! I'd love to do the same thing!"

Nympha and Katou jumped on Growlette's idea. Mamariel and Etheria nodded their agreement.

If the mothers joined the kid's space, the babysitters would be free of their burden.

Wise, Medhi, and Porta were so overwhelmed they actually gave Growlette a hug.

"Growlette, you're the best! You're an awesome mom! I'm gonna call you Mama Growlette now!"

"I'm so touched! So grateful! Would you let me call you Mother, too?"

"Growlette, you're a great mama! I respect you!"

"What? You guys wanna be my kids? Heck, I don't mind! I've already got five; what's one or two or three more? Ah-ha-ha!"

The tough-cookie beastkin took this all in stride.

"So if the three of you are my kids now, you'll join me in the kid's corner!"

""""Huh?""""

All three faces froze, their expressions blank.

While they stood stunned, Growlette picked up the three of them like it was nothing and walked off. "Mom!" "I wanna hug!" "Me too!" Her actual children scurried after, and the other parents and children followed.

"If that's where you guys are headed, then you're definitely gonna end up watching the kids... Good luck, everyone."

Masato clapped his hands together, bowing after them.

The second-round bracket read as follows:

Match 1: The Hero's Mother Mamako vs Devil Mother Invi
Match 2: Android Mother Mechatte vs Elf Mother Chaliele
Match 3: Suspicious Mother Sorente vs Giant Mother Kaide
Match 4: Mysterious Mother Hahako vs Ninja Mother Kunoichiko

A tournament of sixteen would have four rounds in all. They were already in the quarterfinals.

Victory here would advance the mom to the semifinals. Victory there, to the final. And then the crown. The word *win* was on everyone's lips, and it was hard not to feel the pressure.

The mothers gathered in the waiting room all seemed to be looking for ways to alleviate the stress.

Except Mamako.

"Chaliele, do you have a moment? I had a little time this morning, so I baked some cookies. Would you like one?"

"Y-you're baking before a match? That's...some impressive confidence. Hats off to you."

She was acting exactly like she always did.

One mother was watching her intently—the one in the suspicious silver-masked robe, Sorente.

The two girls inside were whispering furiously.

"This time we have to get it riiiight. No more failures like yesterdaaay."

"Yeah, it was our fault for totally forgetting she can nullify all status effects. This time, we'll use a more direct physical attack to rob Mamako Oosuki of her freedom, allowing us to make our move. The perfect plan."

"Yes, yeeees, stop taaaalking. Start waaalking."

Sorente began moving. The moment Chaliele left to get a drink ready, they sidled over to Mamako.

"Mamakooooo, do you have a momeeeent?"

"Oh, you're…Sorente, was it? You gave me that lovely tea yesterday."

"You're weeeelcome. It didn't quite turn out like we expeeeected. Shaaame… Anywaaay…"

Sorente pulled a pendant out from under her robe.

The pendant had the kanji for *mom* written on it upside down. Very disrespectful.

"You see… Masato asked us to give you this preeesent."

"Ma-kun?! For me?!"

"W-w-wow, you sure went for thaaat… You're leaning so far forwaaard!"

"I mean, it's a present from Ma-kun! But… Why would he ask you…?"

"He forgot to hand it oooover. Buuut he's busy working in the broadcast booth. He doesn't have time to bring it here himseeeelf. So he asked uuuus."

"Geez, he really should have just done it in person… But I understand. He was just embarrassed! I'm sure that's why. Hee-hee."

"Right, riiiight. That interpretation wooorks. Sooo…take iiit!"

"Certainly. Thank you!"

Mamako took the pendant and hung it from her neck without the least bit of suspicion. "Oh… This symbol… I feel like I've seen it before…"

"You're imagining iiiit. Byeeee!" Sorente hastily fled the scene.

Once they were in the hall outside the waiting room, their scheme was complete.

"Mwa-ha-haaaa. That went weeeell."

"Looks like it. Mamako Oosuki suspected nothing! She has no idea there's a ghost we captured sealed inside that pendant, and the moment it's released, it will bind her to the spot! ...And we're not about to tell her, of course."

"We just have to be careful to pick the right time to release iiiit! Mwa-ha-haaa!"

"Now that Mamako Oosuki is dealt with...we just have to figure out which of these other mothers is the unidentified unique personage..."

"Sadlyyyy...we don't have time to investigaaate... I wonder who it iiiis..."

The two girls inside Sorente looked around the tense waiting room.

Standing behind them was the mysterious Hahako. She was staring directly at them, but they never noticed.

It was almost time for the first match. But trouble was already rearing its ugly head.

"Masato! You've abandoned your party again!" *Grrr!*

"Hey! You can't just strangle people like— Gah!"

"You're pathetic. It makes me want to punish you." *Twist, twist.*

"W-wait, what? Not my butt— Ahhhhh!"

"Masato..." *Sniff.*

"Wh-whoa! Porta's about to cry?! Don't cry! It's gonna be okay! W-we're all here for you! Right, Shiraaase?"

"So you agree to handle the babysitting instead of these three girls?"

"No, absolutely not." He was very firm on this point.

Growlette had hauled them away, but the girls had managed to escape. They'd come rushing to the broadcast booth.

Standby. Mike switch on.

"Okay, time to get the second day of this tournament started! I hope you're all excited!"

"Today we'll be seeing the second round of matches. Look forward to more passionate displays from our lineup of mothers."

"Please cheer for all the mamas! I'll cheer, too!"

"Sheesh, they've already stolen the mic...," grumbled Masato. "What else are friends for?"

With the three girls on commentary, the tournament hall erupted.

But then a chorus of adorable cries came from the kid's area. "Hi!" "Hiii!" "Just act like you don't see them!" Ears twitching, tails wagging, wings flapping, the children gathered in front of the booth and were politely ignored.

The mothers who'd lost in the first round were clustered together, busy chattering away, leaving their children to whoever was in charge.

It was time.

Masato surreptitiously swiped the mic back from the girls and said, "Time for the first match! Here come our contestants! If Mamako Oosuki could please try to enter calmly without unnecessary excitement... A dignified entrance, please!"

That was important, so he emphasized it.

"Oh my! Ma-kun! You can just call me Mommy like you always do! No need to be embarrassed! Hee-hee!"

Just having him call her name had been enough to put Mamako at maximum excitement. "Ma-kun! Your mommy's in a match!" "I just said not to do that exact thing!" She was jumping up and down onstage, making everything jiggle again.

Then came her opponent, the devil mother, Invi.

"My, my, what a display... I feel left out. I'll have to seduce Masato and make him *my* boy! Hahhh..."

The way she licked her lips was unsettling. This mother was a salacious devil.

She had horns on her head and bat wings sprouting from her back. From her rear grew a tail like a dominatrix's whip. Every bit as curvy as Mamako herself, said curves were crammed into a skintight outfit built for S & M.

Everything about her reeked of criminal behavior. She blew a kiss in Masato's direction.

"Wh-what the—?!" Masato turned red despite himself, which he regretted.

Faced with this display of indecency, Mamako did the natural thing and started chain blowing kisses his way. Masato ignored this.

Both contestants were onstage.

"Uh… So let's decide the contents of this match. Who's on draw box duty?"

"I'll do it!" squealed Porta, who was promptly vetoed by Wise and Medhi: "Masato's turn." "Masato, you're up."

"Thanks to the tyranny of the majority, I am now on duty, so gimme a second to get there."

Masato jumped down from the booth, picked up the box, and went onstage.

The rights to draw for the match content went to whoever had ranked the highest in the prelims. Which meant…

"Now, Mamako Oosuki… Huh?"

When he got closer, he realized she was wearing a weird pendant. He'd never seen that before. It looked terrible on her…and the strange symbol on it bugged him…

However.

"Geez, Ma-kun! Don't treat me like a stranger! I'm your mommy, so you can act all normal!"

"Augh, back off! I'm working here! Just…draw the thing!"

The audience members were all watching. Now was the time to be professional, to ignore any distractions.

She drew…

Shopping + α

Shopping, but no ordinary shopping.

According to the girls in the booth, starting with Wise:

"Shiraaase, what exactly is Shopping + α?"

"They will be given a set budget to purchase necessary supplies for the home. Naturally, they need to purchase modestly priced, high-quality items…but that's not all."

"So what else is required…?" asked Medhi.

"Do they need to earn a bonus?" wondered Porta.

"That's correct. When paying for the items purchased, they must entice the clerk to throw in a little extra."

Aha.

"This match will be held not in the tournament hall, but Meema's shopping district, so someone will have to go with them and officiate."

"I'll do it!" "Masato will." "Masato, you're up."

"I agree that Masato is right for the job. Please prepare yourself."

That clinched it. "Argh... Just pushing all the work on me..." It was good to be relied upon, though. He chose to look at it that way.

"Oh, right! I need to thank you, Ma-kun."

"Huh? For what?"

"Now, now, Masato. No time for chitchat. We're here."

With Mamako and Invi in tow, they reached the Meema shopping district.

It was exactly like any other row of shops. A narrow street with storefronts on both sides selling food and daily necessities. The staff behind the counters wore friendly smiles; it had that comfortable neighborhood vibe of a place that had been exactly like this for years now.

"Here we are... Ahem, broadcast booth, do you copy?" Masato asked.

"Loud and clear!"

"A big screen just appeared onstage, so we can see everything that's happening!"

"Oh yeah? I didn't know they could do that. Wonder if it's some special spell..."

"No, just typical live streaming, like any video website. This is a game world, so we can do that sort of thing easily."

"Even if that's true, at least pretend it's magic! Respect the mood!"

"We can also type comments."

He looked up in time to see letters scroll by: **Masato just checked out Mamako's boobs.**

"Was that you, Medhi?! I did no such thing! They just happened to cross my field of vision!" In fact, he'd been looking at Mamako's pendant, but he'd definitely better be careful about that in the future.

Right. Time to get started.

"This is all incredibly awkward, but... Are you both ready to go?"

"Yes! Mommy's ready! With you by my side, I can do anything!"

"I'm ready as well. I'm excellent at shopping. My victory is assured. Hahhh."

Both were carrying baskets—very eco-friendly.

"Right, then. Positions, please. Ready... M-mom it!"

That incredibly embarrassing cry started the match.

The first to move was the devil mother, Invi. "Let's go, Masato!" "Yikes?!" She spread her wings, hoisted Masato into the air, and flew to her destination: the grocery store. A middle-aged man stood behind the counter.

"Welcome, welc— Yikes?! Y-y-you're..."

"Helloooo, Mr. Grocer. Thanks for yesterday."

When Invi landed in front of him, the man hastily grabbed a daikon. He was armed with a vegetable. Ready for battle.

"He sure seems...defensive."

"My round-one battle was also shopping. We came here yesterday, too...and he gave me such a lovely deal. Hahhh."

"I may have let myself get bewitched once, but not today!"

The grocer seemed ready to even the score.

Far from giving her a little bonus, he seemed ready to run her out. But Invi simply did her shopping like she belonged there, looking over the rows of fruits and vegetables...

And then her hand stopped on a bitter melon.

"Oh, that's a good one... So thick and hard and...ribbed. Ohhhh, it's magnificent. It's driving me wild. *Smooch.*"

After caressing the surface of the fruit, she pressed it to her lips with a rapturous smile. *Crap... I shouldn't be watching this...*, Masato thought, but he was unable to tear his eyes away.

Already hunched over, the grocer barked, "Th-that's your dinner tonight? Then pay up! One hundred and fifty mum!"

"Yes, yes, here you go... Oh!" Invi tripped on nothing and bumped into the grocer's arm.

Her deviant devil-mother chest pressed up against him, yielding.

"Auuuughhhh! Th-this sensatiiiiiion!!"

"Oh, I'm so sorry. I'm feeling a little faint."

"F-faint? Th-then you'd better get some nutrition! Here! Take this! And these, too!"

He threw the daikon into Invi's basket, along with some eggplants and cucumbers that were close at hand.

"Oh my! That's so much! You've helped me out again! Thaaank you."

Smooch.

"Aiiiieeee?! Hngg..."

The kiss to his ear knocked him right out.

Invi had purchased a bitter melon for 150 mum and received a daikon, an eggplant, and a cucumber for free, a bonus worth a total of five hundred mum.

Moments later, the grocer prostrated himself as his wife scolded him. "You can't give away our merchandise!" "I know! Sorry!" But that was neither here nor there.

As Masato stared in horror, Invi came sashaying over to him.

"This is a devil mother's skill, Seductive Shopping. What do you think?"

"I...see. It's definitely a bit problematic, but... Well done. I guess that puts you in the lead..."

"Oh, that's not what I mean. I mean, don't you want a mom like me?"

Invi wrapped herself around Masato's arm, squeezing. "Eeaughh?!" When this wasn't his own mom but another mom, the sensation was...!

And then his actual mother came bursting in.

"Ah! Ma-kun! There you are!"

"Eep?! No! This wasn't my idea!"

Masato immediately freed himself from Invi's clutches, prostrating himself. "Ah! What am I doing?" The grocer had done the same to his wife—apparently, the habit was catching.

"Um, Mom... I mean, Mamako Oosuki... Argh, screw professionalism. I'm just gonna keep calling you Mom."

"Okay! I am your mommy, after all!"

"Invi's already done her shopping and earned a bonus. What's your plan?"

"Naturally, I'm going to try my best! Just you watch!"

Mamako put her basket on her arm and headed into the grocer's.

Back at the tournament hall...

"Geez, what is Masato doing...? Oh, Porta, want some cookies?"

"Yes! I'd love some! Thank you so much!"

"Here, Ms. Shiraaase, have some, too," offered Medhi. "Mamako made them."

"She did? Handmade by Mamako! Don't mind if I do."

The broadcast booth was enjoying tea and cookies.

Meanwhile, on-screen, Mamako was hustling toward the grocer.

Watching from the shadows of the entrance tunnel, Sorente made their move.

"Now! Activate the creature sealed in the pendant!"

"You don't need to tell meeeee! Goooo!"

Under that robe, the person on top was capable of controlling millions of undead monsters at once. She activated her power, and…

…as Mamako stood before the grocer, a change swept over her.

"Oh? …Oh my!"

A number of tentacles suddenly stretched out from the pendant, wrapping themselves around Mamako's body.

The tentacles swiftly peeled off her apron, then her armor, then her dress, even her bra and panties…

They folded all this equipment and handed it to Masato. Here you go!

"Uh, thanks… No, wait, what the hell?!"

They had placed her underwear on top of the pile, so Masato hastily hid those inside her dress. More importantly…

The tentacles were busy consuming Mamako. They had her chest and nether regions—basically the most important bits—safely covered, but their encroachment was spreading across her supple skin.

And looking closer, a pair of horns was growing from her head—and wings from her back.

At this rate, it looked like Mamako was ready to turn into something else entirely…

Watching this, Invi whispered, "This is…a type of ghost that robs someone of her freedom and transforms them into a devil. A type of creature made by devils, released here and there around the world. Incidentally, these are made by the official tourism board."

"More tourism promotion?! There's a limit to how aggressive advertising should be!"

"The declining birth rate affects devils, too… We need to increase our numbers somehow."

"That does sound like a challenge, but can you find a way to do it that doesn't actively harm other races?!"

At any rate, it seemed they had to take the devil's word for it.

"So…my mom's turning into a devil? …M-Mom?!"

"My, my! This pendant is a frisky one! There, there. Good tentacle. Now, behave!" *Pat, pat.*

"Why are you petting the tentacles?!"

Actually, it seemed to be working quite well.

Mamako was stroking the pendant like she had a sobbing child's head buried in her chest.

The tentacles soon stopped their advance. Like they'd fallen asleep, they stopped moving, and Mamako's transformation halted as well.

Her body was covered, but not with clothes. The ratio of bare skin to tentacle covering was about ninety-eight to two, like body paint you didn't dare look directly at.

The horns and wings were soft and flimsy, like a cicada that had just molted.

Despite this, her expression hadn't changed at all; Devil Mamako had that same warm smile.

"Mom… Look at you…"

"This is… Oh, I get it! You wanted to make sure I'd win, so you made sure I'd be dressed as boldly as Invi!"

"Er… What?"

"I'm a little embarrassed, but this is a present from you, Ma-kun, right? Mommy will do her best to wear it well! Okay, off I go!"

"What?! What present?! I didn't give you any presents! Wait, come back and explain… Or just wait! You can't go shopping dressed like… Augh!"

It was too late to stop her. Devil Mamako had charged in.

The grocer saw a new devil approaching and instantly went tense. "Leave this one to me!" "R-right, good idea!" The grocer's wife tapped in.

"You're facing me this time! Do your worst!"

"Oh, one hundred mum for a head of cabbage? That's such a bargain! I'll have to get one."

"Right! One cabbage!"

The cabbage was tossed into her basket. "Here's your payment!"

"Thanks for coming!" One hundred mum handed over.

"Then I'll be on my way!" *Smile.*

"Sure thing! Come again!" *Smile.*

Devil Mamako and the grocer's wife traded smiles. Mamako turned to leave... "Waaaait a second!" The grocer's wife stopped her. "Hang on! You aren't even gonna ask for any kind of bonus?! And all you're buying is cabbage?! That doesn't make any sense!"

"Oh, what's wrong with it?"

"Everything! You know full well the whole point of this contest is to get as many extras as you can... And!"

The wife's gaze turned to Masato.

"The boy there's your son, right? I heard him call you Mom!"

"Yes, that's right! He's my son. His name's Ma-kun!"

"Don't introduce me dressed like that! ...But, uh, y-yeah, hi. I'm her son."

"I thought so... He's a growing boy! You can't leave here with just a head of cabbage! You need something more nutritious! Here!"

The grocer's wife grabbed some carrots and potatoes and tomatoes and put them in Devil Mamako's basket.

"Goodness, so many! It's getting rather heavy."

"Oh, then I'll carry it for you. Gimme that basket."

"Why, thank you! Here."

Masato took the basket from Mamako, feeling like this was probably the right thing to do. It was packed full and definitely heavy.

At a glance, the extra veggies were more than twice what Invi had earned.

"Now, how much do I owe—?"

"Don't be ridiculous!" said the grocer's wife. "Those veggies all hopped in your basket of their own free will. Since they volunteered for it, it's only fair I foot the bill."

"Oh? But..."

"Really, it's fine! ...Ma'am, this is a neighborhood store. Our business doesn't run on profit; it runs on community spirit. We do this for the greater good! Parents come shopping, their kids quietly take the baskets for them... Seeing something as lovely as that, anyone would do the same! Right, everyone?"

She addressed Masato's group as they began to leave. When they turned to look...

...they found a man in boots and a waterproof apron, a woman who smelled like croquettes, and an old man carrying individually wrapped side dishes.

"Such a lovely family! You've gotta try our fish!" *Toss.*

"So good of you to help your mother like this! Here, the butcher's special croquettes!" *Toss.*

"Gotta raise a good boy like this right! Take these!" *Toss.*

"Er, um..."

So much food it couldn't possibly fit in the basket, all tossed on top of the pile.

Finally...

"Your mom might dress like a deviant, but you keep treating her right."

The grocer's wife slapped Masato on the back and went back inside. "Geez, you just gave her a lot." "You got a problem with that?" "Nope. That's what I love about you." The grocer couple seemed to have made up. May they live happily ever after.

As for the results!

Mamako had purchased a cabbage for one hundred mum.

And been given potatoes, carrots, tomatoes, lettuce, fish that looked like mackerel, croquettes, and some side dishes that clearly were worth over two thousand mum in all.

Meanwhile, the devil mother had only managed around five hundred mum in extras. This was clearly Mamako's victory...except for one thing.

Masato frowned in thought, then made a call.

"Hello, Shiraaase? Do you read me?"

"Loud and clear, and I'm aware of the situation."

"Then I'll make it quick. Is there any rule against obtaining the bonus because the mother had her child with her?"

"Absolutely not. Having children with them is the essence of a mother."

"Still... I'm supposed to be here to do live-on-the-scene commentary, not to shop. I'd be surprised if Invi accepted this..."

"But I do, Masato," Invi said.

The naughty mother who lived to entice and pilfer looked almost happy, like the storm had passed.

"This battle's victor is Mamako—no, this victory belongs to both of you."

"...You're sure?"

"I am. I get along with my son, but...he would never go shopping with me. 'It's embarrassing being with you,' he says."

"Well, yeah, if you acted like that, he'd be mortified."

"And yet, when Mamako took devil form, you accepted it and even identified yourself as her son... How did you ever manage to raise a boy this considerate? I find myself completely defeated."

"It's not like I wanted to!! Even I was kinda impressed with my fortitude!" Masato yelped, wiping the tears the memories brought forth.

But the match was decided.

The Shopping + α battle may have skirted the line of broadcast standards, but with her victory, this match was— "Now's our chance to atta— Wait, she's not tied up?!" "Mm?" "Plan faaaailed! Retreat at oooonce!" He felt like he noticed something silver come dashing in and out in the blink of an eye. But whatever, the match was settled.

Back in the hall, the next match started without even a moment for him to rest.

Mamako had reverted to her usual appearance, and she and Invi headed for the kid's area. They were greeting other mothers, letting the kids run wild, chattering happily away.

Masato stepped into the broadcast booth to find an empty cookie tray.

"...No one saved any for me?"

"It's the moment you've been waiting for! Time for the next match! All contestants, assemble!"

"Hey! Where are my cookies?! I've been through the wringer, and my body is craving sugar!"

With all those extra calories, Wise's live commentary was very energetic. The second match began!

Two mothers appeared from the entrance tunnel.

First, the elf mother, Chaliele—looking every bit as serene as one would expect an elf to be.

Then the android mother, Mechatte—her glamourous metallic body gleaming, several flying drones in tow.

A mother from a race known as the Sages of the Forest and a mother who was all machine. Two mothers from opposing worlds, clashing.

"The second match of round two brings together two very different mothers. This should be an interesting battle!"

"A battle between nature and science! I'm so excited!"

"Masato, the draw box."

"I really am just the odd jobs guy, huh? …Fine, I'll do it."

Leaving the mics to the girls, he hustled down to the stage with the box.

During the prelims, the elf mother had placed second, and the android mother, fourth. So it was Chaliele's right to draw. "Chaliele, if you would." "I wonder what it'll be…" She pulled a slip of paper out of the box.

CLEANING (LEVEL 99)

A cleaning battle at the highest difficulty level. What that meant, Masato had no clue.

"Uh, broadcast booth, explain!"

"Righto… Shiraaase! What kinda battle is this?" asked Wise.

"Essentially, they'll be cleaning the air itself. Even when air looks clean, it may have cold viruses, pollen, and other matter suspended in it. Children are especially ill-equipped to deal with these things, and any household with small children should take precautions."

"I see. That sounds like a battle that will test a mother's capacity."

"It sounds so hard! Good luck, everyone!"

"At this point, we will be releasing the air they'll be cleaning. It will be confined to the space above the stage."

Faintly cloudy air began to hiss through the gaps in the stage's wood floors. With pollution included, the area over the stage soon reeked of household smells.

But they had arranged it so this air would not reach the kid's area around the stage—don't worry.

"Then it's time to begin!" "Ready?" "Mom it!"

The girls' shouts got the match underway.

Both moms were frowning, clearly displeased. Chaliele was covering her face with a grass-green handkerchief. Mechatte had automatically equipped a metallic antidote mask.

"This...is certainly not an environment we can allow children to breathe in."

"We must deal with it immediately."

"First come, first served. If you don't mind..."

Chaliele pulled an acorn-like seed out of her pocket and tossed it on the ground nearby.

Then she chanted, "Seed of Mother Forest... If you, too, are a mother, you'll understand. We all want our children to grow up breathing clean, fresh air... If you understand these feelings, lend me your power."

Her plea, filled with love, hit home.

The seed cracked open, extending roots and a bud...and growing in the blink of an eye into a giant tree that was over thirty feet tall.

This was all so sudden, it stunned the crowd and the girls in the booth. Well, not Shiraaase.

"Th-that's...massive...," stammered Wise.

"Trees from the elf forest have a powerful purification effect," explained Shiraaase. "It seems she's using that to cleanse the air. A very elven way of doing things."

The tree's leaves were inhaling the unclean air and releasing healthy air instead. The air around the tree was getting visibly cleaner.

Chaliele took a deep breath and smiled.

"This is the elf mother air-cleansing skill of elf village legend, Mother Forest's Breath... Mechatte, what do you think?"

"You've added the smell of the forest, and I'm detecting negative ions. This air is definitely quite healthy—refreshing, even. Perfect for raising children."

"Of course, of course. Hee-hee. Then I've won?"

"I'll admit you've put me in a tough spot."

The android mother looked up at the mystic tree, her expression grim. Had she lost?

But then:

Looking up at the tree from the kid's space, Masato wondered aloud, "Uh… But a tree this big would never fit inside a house, right?"

"""""Oh.""""""

Chaliele, Mechatte, the audience, everyone in the kid's area, and even Shiraaase all turned and gaped at Masato. "Uh… Did I say something weird…?" Nope, not at all.

The effect of this tree was certainly something everyone desired…

…but growing a tree indoors was not a viable solution for the average home.

Which meant…

"U-um… Oh, Masato! You shouldn't have said anything!" Chaliele wailed.

"I appreciate your assistance, Masato. This gives me a chance to counterattack."

Mechatte stepped forward.

"Mode: Air Cleanliness!"

Her drones docked onto her back, transforming into a very high-tech-looking fan. The fan began turning, drawing in the dirty air around her.

Watching from the sidelines, Masato got so worked up, he grabbed the edge of the stage.

"Whoa! This is turning into a real sci-fi battle! I bet this next part's gonna be really cool! Are you gonna use lasers?!"

He was sure of it. Lasers. Like, really big ones. Huge.

The armor under Mechatte's armpits opened with a *clang!* "An opening! And next comes…" It kind of looked like a nozzle! These nozzles…

…produced a gentle breeze.

"Just ventilation?!"

"I am equipped with an air purifier, a humidifier, and a dehumidifier, as well as an air coolant system. This is the power of a mechanical mother: the Mama Conditioner System! This skill is called the M.C.—the MamaCon!"

The filters inside her body were very high quality, catching all the unwanted particles in the air. And it was an automatic process, so no hands were required. She could produce clean air at any time.

And since the mother herself was conditioning the air, it didn't take up any space in the room.

On a hot day, you could just run over to Mom and enjoy the cool air. On a cold day, you could run to Mommy and enjoy the heat.

Faced with this functionality, Chaliele calmly admitted defeat. "Oh my. I suppose I've lost." The match was over.

"Mechatte wins the second match!" Shiraaase declared.

The crowd roared. "They were both amazing!" "I'm so impressed!" The mothers in the kid's area applauded, too.

But not Masato:

"She made it seem like she was going to use some spectacular super-move, and it was just an AC... What a waste of a mecha..."

"According to our data, Mechatte was originally designed as combat weaponry, but after the war, she was converted from an assault-type unit to a life-support unit. Raising children for adults preoccupied with the rebuilding effort, ensuring all could live in happiness."

"Yeah, I know peace is the answer! But...still!"

Some people would just never understand how a boy's mind worked. He stamped his foot in frustration.

But before he could cool off or vent his frustration, the third match began.

"Okay, Ma-kun! Next match!" *Grin.*

"Oh yeah... Why are you right here? Since when...?"

"Everyone else is enjoying the match with their children, so Mommy just wanted to be with you, too... And here come the contestants! Everyone, please give them a round of applause!"

"And now you're an announcer, too?!"

The next round's contestants were emerging from the tunnel.

First up was the giant mother, Kaide.

"Hokay! Here we go!"

Towering fifteen feet high, she came skipping into the room. Boobs so big even an adult couldn't wrap their arms around them swaying. The earth shaking.

She was followed by the suspicious mother, Sorente.

"Yes, yeeeees. Helloooo. I'm not suspicious at aaaaall."

Covered in a silver-masked robe, this contestant stood at over six feet tall.

Taller than all the other mothers but still extremely small when standing next to Kaide.

Maybe they could get accidentally stepped on and squished to death.

Part of Masato genuinely meant that. They were his enemies, after all.

He reached into his pocket and took out the pendant he'd swiped from Mamako.

There was a logo on it that looked like the kanji for *mom* upside down.

I finally remembered... This is the mark of the Libere Rebellion.

The same mark appeared on the coats Amante and Sorella wore. No wonder it looked familiar. This pendant was an enemy item.

They'd tricked Mamako into believing it was a present from Masato, convinced her to wear it, and turned her into a devil...and as a result, Masato had been forced to endure the humiliation of going shopping with his mother dressed like that... Just remembering made him angry.

"Now, now, Ma-kun. No time to get lost in thought! They need to draw the match contents!"

"Huh? ...Oh yeah, right..."

"The one job we've left you, Masato. Knock 'em dead!"

"The three of us and Mamako will handle the commentary."

"Masato! Good luck with the draws!"

"And I'm sure you're aware that Sorente is..."

"Being kept under surveillance. Right. Even though they've caused plenty of trouble already... Whatever."

Masato forced himself to choke it down. He was pushed out of the broadcast booth, and then be carried the draw box up onto the stage.

In the prelims, Kaide had ranked thirteenth, and Sorente, ninth. Which meant...

"Sorente, here."

"Yes, yeeees. Gotta draaaaw."

Masato scowled furiously at them as he angrily held out the box, but Sorente withdrew a slip of paper, seemingly oblivious to this.

LAUNDRY DX

What could make laundry deluxe? Masato had no clue. This was straight-up enigmatic.

He also didn't care.

"Then I'll just go back. I'm sure Shiraaase will explain the details. My job here is done."

He put the box under his arm and headed listlessly away, but—

"Masatoooo. Waaaait."

—Sorente grabbed him by his jacket collar.

"Uh... Would you mind letting go?"

"Laundry Deluuuuxe means we have to do amaaaaazing laundry, riiiight? Make it sooooo! ...*Hyaaaah!*"

"Aughhh?!"

They'd yanked the jacket right off him.

And then Sorente reached for his shirt.

"Wh-what the hell?! Stop that! ...W-wait... I'm feeling very weak... I can't resist... No!"

"Mwa-ha-haaaa! Just hold stiiiill!"

Sorella must be using her debuff skill. Masato was helpless! "I'll be taking thaaat!" "Aiiieee!" His shirt was gone! He was naked from the waist up! Mortifying!

Masato had been running around all day, so his top had a lot of sweat soaked into it. Not quite to the level of being dirty, but...

"This shirt needs waaaaashing! Ooooone...twooooo...threeee!" Sorente grunted and shook the shirt a few times.

"Neeeext step..."

"First, you debuff the dirt's sticking power and shake it out," the other person in the robe started muttering. "Then I'll use my reflection skill to—"

"Don't explain iiiiit! Just shut up and woooork!"

"Okay, I'm done." "Gooood! All doooone."

They appeared to be done already.

Sorente held it up proudly.

"Laundry compleeeete! Go ahead, check iiiit!"

"Check what?"

"Ohhh... Riiiight... You would struggle with thaaat. But a mother with any degree of skill would get iiiit... Can we get one to cheeeck?"

"Huh? Wha—? Me?" Masato's shirt was placed in Kaide's massive hand.

The giant mother stared down at it and then went pale.

"This—! ...L-lemme just test it!"

She started rubbing the shirt against the stage. "Hey!" Doing that would make Masato's shirt dirty...but it didn't.

The dirt that got on the shirt was forcibly ejected, and it stayed clean.

"Bu—? How...?"

"This shirt will cast off any dirt! It can never get dirty again! Because it can't get dirty, you never need to wash it, and the fabric never gets damaged! This is truly flawless laundry!"

"Exaaaactly. Mwa-ha-haaa... Sooooo, giant moooother... What sort of laundry skills do you have that can match thiiiis?"

"I—I... The only skill I've got just allows me do thirty loads of regular laundry at once... There's no way I could ever win, no matter how hard I try! WAHHHHHHH!"

"Then you loooose, and I wiiiiin. Thanks for plaaaaying!"

Sorente snatched the shirt from Kaide's hand and left the stage.

Nothing had been made official, but the outcome was clear.

Their laundry skill was so powerful, the audience forgot to cheer. The mothers watching were as stunned as the crowd.

The only sound left was Kaide's sobs. "Mom!" "Don't cry!" The giant's child and Mamako ran over to comfort her, but the waterfall of tears kept flowing.

But no amount of crying would change the results.

Sorente's overwhelming victory had lowered the curtain on the third match…

Wait.

"…Ah! Why am I just standing here?! Give me back my shirt!"

Masato went running off, chasing Sorente.

Masato burst through the tunnel into the waiting room, but there was no sign of Sorente.

Instead, he found the mysterious mother, Hahako. She had his shirt in her hands, so clean it was like a brand-new shirt. She was staring gloomily at it.

"Er… Um, excuse me? Is that shirt…mine, perhaps?" he asked timidly.

Hahako just nodded mysteriously and pointed at the garbage can in the corner.

"So they just threw my shirt away?! Argh, so mad!"

What should he do to them? Catch up with them and beat them to…? No, he'd be the one to get beaten. His anger gave way to a shudder.

Meanwhile, Hahako unfolded the shirt and came closer. She took Masato's arm and slipped it through the sleeve, helping him put it on.

"Wait, uh… I can do this myself…"

Hahako shook her head mysteriously and kept going. She did all the buttons up for him, too. "Hey!" She even tucked the hem of the shirt into his pants and then straightened the collar.

"Uh… Th-thanks. Thank you."

This was so awkward, but he felt he at least owed her his thanks.

Hahako bowed her head. She seemed satisfied. Her body wiggled from side to side like she was enjoying this.

"………!"

Then Hahako seemed to get an idea. She ran over to the bench on the far wall and sat down.

Then she patted her lap. Repeatedly. Was that an invitation?

"Um… You mean…a lap pillow?"

She nodded.

Enthusiastically.

She wanted Masato to use her lap as a pillow. "Uh… Thanks for the offer, but..." He tried to refuse politely, and Hahako looked dejected. She even started crying. She really seemed invested in this lap pillow thing.

What now?

Accepting a lap pillow from a total stranger definitely didn't seem like a reasonable option, but...

Who is Hahako anyway?

Shiraaase had not infooormed them of the particulars.

This might be a chance to learn more about her. A once-in-a-lifetime opportunity. In which case...

"Th-then I guess...just for a minute?"

"......!" *Nod, nod.*

Curiosity and the spirit of inquiry overcame his sense of shame. Masato decided to lie down on the bench, softly putting his head on Hahako's lap. And felt...

Ohhh... Definitely a lap pillow...

A little too high. Yet soft, warm, and such a pleasant smell...

And relaxing. More than anything, it felt satisfying. Like bliss seeping directly through his skin into his brain. When she gently rubbed his head, the bliss value doubled.

He closed his eyes and felt the urge to fall asleep, just like...

Exactly like Mamako's mom skill, A Mother's Lap.

"...Huh?!"

Masato jumped to his feet, staring down at the mysterious mother's lap.

This was the lap of a total stranger. Not Mamako's.

But the effect Masato felt was definitely...

Then...Shiraaase's voice crackled over the loudspeaker.

"The fourth match is about to begin. Masato Oosuki, please return to your position. Your mother seems ready to unleash her skill to find you. Return at once."

A Mother's Fangs?

"Yikes, I gotta get back! Uh, so... You heard the lady; I gotta run. Thanks, though! Good luck in your match!"

He turned his back on Hahako and ran off at full speed, as if fleeing the motherly aura that had so perplexed him.

The fourth match was in progress.

Two human competitors had fought their way to this battle and now faced each other.

First was the ninja mother, Kunoichiko, making full use of ninja arts in an outfit that...seemed actually like it would attract quite a bit of attention, really.

"I shall not lose! The whole 'mothers are ninjas' thing may have been improvised, but the kids believed it, so I've got to win for them!"

Meanwhile, her opponent was Hahako, her true nature and identity still shrouded in mystery.

"........."

The category this time was: CLEANING (DANGER LEVEL: MAX). The same as Mamako's first-round battle.

Once again, Masato's real-world room was re-created onstage. They were competing to clean the room while recovering only the hidden items meant for a mother's eyes. If they discovered anything best left unseen, they were out.

The match was already at its climax. The girls in the booth were getting quite worked up.

"I said *The bookshelves!* He's got 'em camouflaged! I swear!"

"Go for any titles that sound excessively academic! They're definitely suspicious!"

"Hrmm... I feel like they're specifically trying to make us find something dangerously sexy...but maybe that's a double blind! ...Buddha, guide my hand!"

Kunoichiko made up her mind and grabbed the encyclopedia. When she opened it...

...she found a calendar filled with drawings of beautiful girls in their underwear. "Whoa?!" "Hell yeah!" "Well done!" As the ninja mother stared in horror, the girls erupted in shouts of victory.

Despite his privacy being violated in the public eye...

...the room's owner remained utterly calm.

Something very weird's going on here.

He was sitting at the edge of the booth, watching closely.

Studying Hahako's every move.

" ......"

She'd finished cleaning and, just like Mamako had in the first round, was using a special mother skill for searching children's rooms, A Mother's Search. Checking every corner of the room…

And then she found something. She suddenly darted forward, picked up the garbage can, and under it…

…was a test from school! The form had a field for parents to sign. This was something he was definitely supposed to show his mother. She was right to find it.

She won.

"And done! The fourth match goes to the mysterious mother, Hahako!" Shiraaase announced.

The cheers were so loud they seemed ready to split the hall in two.

But despite the commotion around him, Masato alone was lost in thought.

She looks just like Mom, has all her skills… How…?

Hahako had turned to gaze up at him. Mamako was staring at him from the kid's space. Masato's eyes went from one to the other, deep in thought…

Masato continued thinking, long after the tournament ended and upon returning to the inn, well into the evening.

Out in the hall, he could hear voices: "Oh, missy!" "Found ya!" followed by "You were looking for us?!" "Aren't there more of them now?!" "There aaare!" A desperate game of tag was unfolding, but even that sound didn't shake him from his reverie.

Elbows on the dining room table, he racked his brain.

"She didn't react to my skill, but she has mom skills…and she looks just like Mom… What could that mean? Ugh, I just don't know!"

"Well, at a time like that, it's best to eat something! Fuel for the brain!"

"Yeah, maybe… Then I guess I will."

A very red bowl of *mapo doufu* was placed in front of him, and he took a heaping spoonful, chowing down. "Mm, so good... Hmm? ...H-H-HOTTTTTTTTTTT!" It was so spicy flames literally shot out of Masato's mouth.

"Oh! A lovely burst of flames! You've got a talent for breath attacks, Masato! You oughta become my kid and aim to be the dragon hero!"

"Huh? Dragon hero?! That sounds awesome! ...But wait, Sammo Hung, since when are you staying at this inn—? Arghhh, the spice is killing meeeeeee! Gaaaaaahhh!"

The dragonewt mother's extra-hot Szechuan cooking had turned his mouth into a furnace. It was definitely leaving permanent burns.

Then...

"Oh my, my. Your mouth is all charred, Masato! You know what this calls for? Some fun time toothbrushing with this vampire mommy! Say ahhh!"

"Huh? Hngggg?!"

Kangoshii, the vampire dressed like a nurse, had appeared quietly behind Masato. She got Masato's mouth open and stuck a toothbrush inside, brushing his teeth for him.

"B-bu—? Dis 'eels goo'!"

"I'm sure it does. It's a lovely feeling. If you were my son, you could do this every day, morning, noon, and night. Mommy would love to brush your teeth for you any time. What do you say?"

The mouth was a highly sensitive sensory organ, and having a mother massage the inside struck him as morally wrong somehow. He had to stop this. "Enough!" "Oh, he ran away." Masato made an emergency exit.

He fled the dining room, into the living room. But there were more mothers waiting there.

Specifically, Mamako. Sitting on the couch, folding Masato's laundry. Perfect.

"Oh, Ma-kun! So much shouting. What happened?"

"You were too busy with my laundry to realize what was happening...probably for the best. It was nothing; don't worry about it."

Masato sat down next to Mamako. Then...

He took a good long look at Mamako's thighs. Not in a weird way. An investigatory gaze.

"Oh my! Ma-kun, do you want a lap pillow? Go right ahead!"

"N-no, I don't, but... Uh, if you're offering, I suppose I could. Just to check something!"

Masato let himself topple over in her direction, resting his head on Mamako's thighs.

"Check something? Like what?"

"Never mind that."

"Awww... Oh, but that reminds me!"

Mamako suddenly began inspecting Masato's shirt carefully.

He was still wearing the shirt Sorente had washed so flawlessly. Mamako had clearly picked up on something...but Masato didn't care. More importantly...

He closed his eyes, letting the sensations of his real mother's lap pillow embrace him.

Mm. Definitely mom's lap pillow.

Soft, warm, relaxing, satisfying, that same inexplicable bliss.

Definitely her. He'd never mistake this feeling. This was A Mother's Lap.

But at the same time, it reminded him of the mysterious mother, Hahako.

It isn't just similar. It's the exact same lap pillow. What does that mean?

He looked up and saw Mamako's face.

But for a moment, it looked like Hahako's.

Questions he had no answers for spun around inside his mind.

The exhaustion of the day and the effect of the lap pillow soon lured Masato to sleep.

DEVIL MAMAKO

SKILLS

SEDUCTIVE SHOPPING
Can bewitch the shop staff into giving discounts and special bonuses.

VITALITY DRAIN
Obtains the energy needed to remain active by stealthily draining selected targets.

STRENGTHS

Boasts the ultimate performance when shopping or dealing with finances. However...

WEAKNESSES

Given her indecent appearance, Masato tries to avoid contact with her. Also, her vitality drain decreases the need to cook, her sexy clothes take extra time to wash, and all that exposed skin means cleaning makes her dirty, so her overall stats are consequently reduced.

STATS

STATS

MATERNITY: 100 / COOKING: 60 / LAUNDRY: 60
CLEANING: 60 / SHOPPING: 150 / COMBAT: 80
MA-KUN: 100

SPECIAL EXPOSURE: 120

Chapter 4 That Lunch Was Made by Mom but Not My Mom.

In the bedroom of the inn, on a bed.

Wise was begging for it.

"Masato... More... Rub it harder..."

"L-like this?" *Rub, rub.*

"More! Even harder! Really get in there and knead it!"

"O-okay, I won't hold back, then... How's this?" *Squeeze!*

"Unhhh! Yes, that's it! That's the spot! It hurts so good!"

Wise let out a soft moan, her body writhing in pleasure and pain. Her hands clutched Masato's, clinging to consciousness.

Tears ran down her flushed cheeks.

Maybe the pain was a bit too much... Masato eased up a little, but Wise shook her head, demanding he keep it up, keep it hard, even harder.

But he couldn't focus on Wise alone.

Medhi was equally demanding.

"Masato, please... Do me, too."

"R-really?"

"Yes... Like you're trying to break me. Shove it all the way in."

"Okay, then. Here goes... Mmph!" *Shove.*

"Mwa... Y-yes! There! Harder... Just shove it in there... Ahhhhh!"

Medhi was lying facedown, and Masato was straddling her, leaning over her body.

Thrusting into her, pressing over and over, her body bucking.

Her hands gripped the sheets, and she let out a pained moan, then went limp, collapsing. She turned toward Masato with a look of ecstasy, her grin a challenge. As if asking if that was all he had, as if daring him to do more.

Masato's pride as a man and his sadistic side both took the bait. If she wanted it...

"Masato! Do me, too! I want more!" Wise wrapped herself around his arms and legs like she couldn't bear waiting any longer.

He was about to switch back to her, but Medhi wrapped herself around his other arm.

"Masato, I'm not satisfied yet. Finish me first."

"Hey! Medhi! I called dibs! Do me first!"

"No, my dibs were still in effect. I want you, Masato."

"Masato! It's my turn!"

Two flushed girls' bodies demanded Masato's attention.

If they wanted him that bad, Masato was—

"Uh, sorry. I need to take a break. My arms are killing me."

Masato threw his lactic-acid-filled arms in the air. His muscles were screaming.

But Wise's and Medhi's demands were not so easily swayed.

"I'm way more beat than you! Just when we thought we were finally free of those kids, they all showed up at the inn and chased us everywhere! My legs are all tired and swollen!"

"I'm suffering, too. I had to pick them up so many times, and now my back is just... Masato. Keep the massage going."

"Yeah! Massage away! Extra attention to the calves!"

So, well, that was the long and short of it.

It was a nice, healthy morning.

Sunshine and children's laugher came streaming in through the windows. Mothers were hanging out the laundry and chattering away.

The three of them were in the room, along with Porta, who was still asleep. "......Mmph-mm..." "Oops, got a little too loud there. Sorry." It was still quite early. Masato patted her cover a bit, hoping to let her sleep longer.

Then he sat down hard on the other bed, specifically to annoy the two girls on it.

"Geez. You're working me to the bone! I'm plenty worn out myself, y'know. I got my own stuff to think about, too."

"Stuff to think about? Like what?"

"New hiding places for his filth, I assume."

"Ohhh, gotcha... So they found 'em all, huh?"

"No! Not that! It's about Hahako."

"Hahako? ...Oh yeah, yeah. The lady who looks just like Mamako."

"There's certainly a startling resemblance. Very different vibes, though... What about her?"

"It isn't just her appearance. She has the exact same skills. Like she's a copy of my mom. So—"

"You want a second mommy to spoil you. I get it."

"A mom on either arm, constantly all over each other... How immoral."

"Nooooo! Absolutely not! I'm serious here. I wanna know exactly who or what she is!"

"Calm down; we know. We were kidding, okay? Just messing with you."

But after they'd calmed him, both girls suddenly looked grim.

"Seriously, though. You really shouldn't talk about other mothers," warned Wise.

"Huh? Why not?"

"If Mamako heard you, she'd get all jealous, and heaven only knows what would happen then...," said Medhi.

"Oh, I think that'll be fine. Mom's..."

But before Masato could finish...

...the door swung open, and Mamako came running in. Each hand held one of Masato's shirts.

"Ma-kun! Can you look at these? I washed your shirts for you! Which is better, the shirt Sorente washed or the shirt Mommy washed with love? Tell me!"

She held up the two in turn and continued to press him for an answer, but she was clearly emphasizing the shirt in her right hand. That was probably the one she'd washed.

Anyway.

"Mom's been like this since yesterday evening. Nothing else seems to get through to her. No point worrying about other things till I deal with this, is there?"

""Makes sense.""

Wise and Medhi gave him looks of great sympathy.

*　　*　　*

The third day of the World Matriarchal Arts Tournament arrived.

The hall was packed to the brim again. Throngs awaiting further dynamic duels.

The kid's area around the stage was bustling. Kaide and Kunoichiko had joined the group from the day before, sparking even more conversation.

There was no need to worry about the children. After all, there was a new babysitter on duty.

"Masato!" "Masatoooo!" "Play with us!" "Pwaaay!" "I wanna hug!"

"How?! How did this happen?!"

He'd been so lost in thought, he'd tuned out his surroundings and carelessly wandered into the kid's area.

The girls were watching with evident delight as Masato was mobbed by children. "Hang in there!" "Best of luck." "Um... Masato! I'm rooting for you!" They were all safely in the broadcast booth. "You could help, y'know!" Their positions had been flipped. And really, this served him right.

"Masato! Play with me! Play with this giant mommy!"

"Gaaahhh!! Get this giant airhead mom off meeee!"

Kaide had scooped up Masato and given him a tight squeeze. "Ack, I'm being buried alive!!" At over fifteen feet tall, the valley between her breasts was deep enough to completely obscure the upper half of Masato's body.

"Ah... What is this? I've never felt like this before... Warm, soft, all around me... This could be dangerous... But seriously, stop! Emergency ejection! Hah!"

He curled himself all the way up and then shoved his way free of Kaide's boobs. Safe!

...Nope. Kunoichiko blocked his way.

"Halt! I saw what you just did. You used the secret ninja art of the Boob Escape!"

"Er, that's one way to put it, but... Can we not?"

"I had no idea you were a ninja, Masato. In which case, you should become my son and train with me! Let's aim to be master ninjas together!"

"Very tempting, but no, thanks! Excuse me!"

Masato tried to make a run for it, but... "Not so fast! Clone Technique!" Kunoichiko made clones of herself, a huge crowd of them surrounding Masato. There was no escape. "Oh, that looks like fun!" "Let me join in." "A power struggle, eh?" "W-wait a sec!!" More mothers were after him! Masato was in trouble!

But never mind his predicament.

"Good morning, everyone. If you could just check your scripts..."

"Sure, sure... Huh? Shiraaase, today's matches—"

"In the scripts. It's time, so please start reading."

"Um, all right... Thank you all for waiting! We've got another exciting day for you!"

"We're about to begin the third round of the tournament! The semifinals!"

"Here come our contestants! A warm round of applause, please!"

The crowd erupted in response. "No one's gonna help?!" The cheers drowned out Masato's plaintive cry.

And from the entrance tunnel...

First up was Mamako. Looking way too good in that apron, she was smiling like always, but today she looked unusually serious. She was carrying a simple lunch box.

Following her was the android mother, Mechatte. Her flying drones were on standby around her. Like Mamako, she stepped onstage carrying a lunch box.

But that wasn't all! Next was the suspicious mother, Sorente. Convinced their silver-masked robe was hiding their real identity, the Heavenly Kings were carrying a lunch box, too.

And finally, the mysterious mother, Hahako. Since she looked far too much like Mamako, 'mysterious' seemed like an understatement. And of course, she was carrying a lunch box, too.

All four mothers—the top contenders—were onstage, each one carrying a lunch box.

Having all hands on deck like this surprised the crowd and the girls in the booth. "Please! Somebody...!" "Shut up, Masato!" "Will you be quiet?" Masato's desperate attempts to escape the mothers were still being ignored.

"Uh… So, Shiraaase, what's going on here?"

"The third round will follow a battle royale–style format. All four competitors will take part at once, and the two who score the highest will advance to the finals."

"This certainly came out of nowhere… Oh, but I suppose this does eliminate the luck of the draw that tournament formats always involve, without resorting to shuffling the opponents around."

"Clever, Medhi. Exactly our intention."

"Then why do all the mamas have lunch boxes? I don't get that! Please infooorm me!"

"For the third round, they'll be battling over making lunches. They've each been given a lunch box and will be filling it with a mother's special cooking, competing for the best arrangement. They have thirty minutes to complete the lunch! If they fail to finish within the allotted time, they'll be immediately disqualified."

"So cooking speed is critical," said Wise.

"But just cooking fast won't be nearly enough, I'm afraid… The kitchen is a mother's battleground. You never know what might happen there to make a mother's head spin. What will happen? …Well, that's up to our contestants."

"In other words, interfering with their opponents is totally on the books? Lovely!" The blackhearted Cleric approved. Everyone pretended not to see the sinister smile on her lovely face.

A giant magic circle appeared onstage. Four kitchen areas were summoned. Each kitchen had a full complement of utensils and seasonings. Additionally, a counter appeared, heaping with meat, fish, and vegetables.

The contestants sprang into action.

Mamako took Kitchen A. Sorente took Kitchen B, across from her.

Hahako was in Kitchen C, next to Mamako. Mechatte was in Kitchen D.

Once each was ready…

"And with that, let the match—"

"No, wait! The kids are all chasing me now, too! Somebody, please! Help!"

"You in the kid's area—Masato! Silence! That type of disruption is not allowed. You're interfering with the match."

"Have you no heart?!"

"Let the match begin! Ready... Mom it!"

As the match started, they hit the switch on the thirty-minute timer in the broadcast booth.

The first thing that happened was that Mamako, seething with rivalry, thrust her lunch box in Sorente's direction.

"Sorente! It's on!"

"Huhhhhh?! Wh-wh-why has she locked onto uuuuus?!"

"N-no way! Does she know who we are?!"

The girls inside Sorente seemed very rattled by this, but Mamako's focus soon shifted to cooking. "First, check the seasonings!"

"I—I think we're goooood... Wheeeeew."

"Yeah. So better take care of her quick."

"Riiiight. Though whether it will wooork... I just don't knoooow. At the very least, I'm going to use my skiiiill."

"Yo, suspicious lady! I heard you being suspicious! I'm not letting that happen!"

"Interference is allooooowed. Go back to the kid's area, Masatooooo! If you want to watch close-up, go aheeeead. Just don't say a woooord. Pleeeease."

"For someone so suspicious, you're weirdly polite!"

"Anywaaaaay... *Hyaaaah!*"

The girl under the robe activated her debuff skill.

But Mamako's movements didn't slow at all. She was swiftly going through the seasonings.

"Arghhhh! Why didn't it do anythiiiing?!"

"There, there. Mom can null all status effects, so it's completely useless! ...But the other two moms are... Huh?"

Masato stopped dead in his tracks. The crowd of children chasing after him caught up and grabbed him, but he caught sight of something:

Hahako was moving smoothly around Kitchen C, completely unaffected. She, too, seemed to be immune to the debuff skill.

Yo, seriously? ...Even that part's just like Mom?

In fact, Hahako's actions were exactly the same as Mamako's.

When Mamako picked up the soy sauce, so did the mysterious mother. If she picked up vegetable oil, Hahako did the same. It was like she was copying her every move...

Then:

"Warning. Warning. Self-destruct program activated. This body will soon explode. Those in the vicinity should exercise caution."

Mechatte's voice sounded far more mechanical than usual.

"Mode: Acro-cleanliness!"

The drones clustered on her back, turning into a cleaning device for cleaning high areas, wings shining with the light of science fluttering rapidly.

She ascended quickly above Kitchen D and exploded, sending scientific fireworks in all directions.

And then she fell toward Masato, smoke pouring out of her. "Seriously?! Augh!" Masato instinctively caught her. He was sure the impact would shatter his arms, but they were still intact.

"M-Mechatte?! Are you okay?! I mean, you don't look okay, but... why'd you suddenly self-destruct?!"

"I'm designed to self-destruct when my functionality is abruptly reduced. It's a holdover from my days as a combat weapon... A fail-safe to prevent me from falling into enemy hands."

"Ugh! The debuff skill did this? ...Why didn't they deactivate a function that dangerous?!"

"It was possible to deactivate it, but..."

What remained of Mechatte's head turned, looking around.

She was surrounded by children, their eyes gleaming. "That was amazing!" "So pretty!" "Do it again!" Apparently, the fireworks had delighted them.

"If it makes children smile, self-destructing isn't so bad. So it was left intact."

"Risking life and limb for a smile is for circus performers, not mothers!"

But Mechatte just smiled, satisfied, and closed her eyes.

One contestant already (self-)eliminated.

It was now the subject of much discussion inside the broadcast booth.

"That got super-over-the-top real quick... Shiraaase, was that self-destruction the kind of trouble you were expecting?"

"Self-destructing while cooking... I understand it's surprisingly common with android mothers."

"I—I don't think it is, actually...," Medhi disagreed.

"But the android audience members are all nodding!"

Porta was right. Every one of the mechanical women in the audience was nodding vigorously. "The children love it!" "I do it all the time." Apparently, it was just an android thing.

Mechatte was carried off on a stretcher, and the match continued.

In Kitchen C, Hahako continued perfectly copying Mamako's actions, working in silence.

In Kitchens A and B, Mamako and Sorente were crackling with mutual hostility.

"I won't lose to you! I'm Ma-kun's mommy!"

"Arghhh... Well, fiiiine! Then we've got no choooice!"

"Exactly! We can't be picky now! We'll do anything to win! Including..."

Sorente jumped down into the kid's area. "Humph!" "Huh?" As Masato gaped, he was hurled up onto the stage.

He rolled all the way to Mamako's feet.

"Oh, Ma-kun! You wanted to be with Mommy that bad?"

"No! This was involuntary! ...Yo, Sorente, or whatever you call yourself! What the heck was that for?"

"What was it foooor? ...What *was* it fooor?"

"Simple! The debuff skill won't hurt Mamako Oosuki... So let the people around her do it! Not bad, huh?"

"I seeee... You want Masatooo...to cause an interfeeeerence."

"What? Like hell I'd do that! Shut up!"

"The mooore the meeeerrier, then! Sooo... Wiiiise, Poooorta...and not that I'm a faaan, but...Medhiiii! Over heeere!"

The booth's response to Sorente's call?

"There they go, being idiots again... That's gonna be a no from us, right, Shiraaase?"

"No. I'll allow it."

"Huh?" Medhi balked. "You will?"

"Children offering to help always makes us happy, even if they slow us down. Happens all the time. This is one type of kitchen trouble. Mothers should be able to handle it."

And that was that.

Shiraaase covered the mic with her hand and whispered, "If they're facing Mamako directly, they may use force. Think of this as an excuse to stage a counterattack. If anything happens, play it by ear."

"Ohhh. That makes more sense."

"They may force us to fight, you mean."

"Th-then I'll support you the best I can! Leave items to me!"

"Cool! Then let's go!"

The girls poured out of the booth.

The audience appeared on board with the kids joining the match. "Good luck helping!" "Interfere with her!" "Uh, never heard a chant like *that* before!"

Mamako's party converged on her.

Vs Suspicious Mother Sorente—FIGHT!

"Well, if Ma-kun and you girls want to help, I'll take all the hands I can get! Let's do this together!"

"Just to be clear, I'm not here to slow you down."

"Masato might just get in the way, but I'll help you!"

"Masato and Wise will probably get in the way, but I will definitely help!"

""Don't you touch a thing, Medhi!""

"Er, um… I'll do my best! I want to help!"

"You all want to heeeelp, but will youuuu? …Just to make sure you doooon't, I'll stack my skiiiill as high as I caaaan!"

And with that languid proclamation, Sorente slowly raised a hand.

A max debuff effect hit them. Mamako was unaffected, but… "Unh!" Masato's stats fell. "Arghhh!" Wise's stats cratered. "Now you've done it!" Medhi's stats plummeted.

Porta's abilities dropped, too.

"Eep?! My Item Creation and Appraise skills are way less effective now!"

"What?! Porta's noncombatant—it shouldn't even affect her!"

"Mwa-ha-haaaa! Taste the power of the ultimate debuuuuuuff!"

"Now Mamako has four shackles on her... But...this is still Mamako Oosuki we're dealing with..."

"We need a contingency on our contingencyyyy. Let's use the ultimate anti-mom super-attack speeeeell! One, twoooooo..."

""...*Spara la magia per mirare... Sigillo Madre!*""

The two Heavenly Kings inside Sorente chanted together, their spell targeting Mamako.

"Anti-mom magic?! What in the—? No, whatever the effect, Mom'll negate it somehow."

But instead, Mamako was suddenly surrounded by smoke.

"Hmm?"

Masato reflexively turned toward her and saw...

...an extremely tiny mother, looking very serious.

Every bit of her was tiny. Not shrunk—infantilized. She looked to be about five years old. Mamako was now very short and very young. Even her clothes were child-sized.

"Hmm...... Hmm?"

Masato did a double take, exchanged horrified glances with the rest of the party, then did a third take. Still true:

His mother was now a child.

Mamako's age was suddenly reduced! She became Child Mamako!

"Hmm...... Gaaaahhh?! What in the—?!"

Masato was so surprised that his nose was running. "Wh-what the hell?!" Wise's jaw was on the floor like an idiot. "Um? Um? Um?!" Medhi couldn't stop blinking. "Tiny Mama is so cute!" Porta seemed rather pleased.

Sorente were delighted.

"We did iiiiit! We actually did iiiiit!"

"If she's no longer a mother, her motherly power dies, too! With that in mind and a lot of training, we finally managed the ultimate spell! Even Mamako Oosuki can't beat that!"

The two Heavenly Kings' spell had overcome Mamako's defensive equipment.

"H-hey, wait! This is too much! It's definitely cheating!"

"A reeeal mother can still cook no matter what problems might ariiiise. That's the point of this maaaatch."

"W-well..."

They looked toward the booth, but Shiraaase sat in silence, biting her lip. Sorente was right. She was forced to allow it.

"Then it's seeeettled! As is the maaaatch! ...I bet Mamako can't cook at all noooow!"

"And it's not just her body that changed! The mom seal spell made her a child on the inside, too! Not that I need to explain that! Heh-heh-heh!"

"Wh-what?!"

If Mamako was a child inside...

"Ma-kun! Stay focus on da match! Dun worry! Mommy's here! Iss gonna be okay!"

"Uh... She seems like herself?"

""Huh? ...How?!""

No matter what form her body took, a mother's mind remained wholly unchanged. They could relax and continue the tournament.

The match was well underway. And there was a time limit—they only had twenty minutes left.

Time was of the essence, but so was prudence.

"...Mom, listen. About Sorente—"

"Oh, I know. Dat's Amante 'n' Sorella!"

"You noticed? ...Well, sure. Anyone would."

"Amante 'n' Sorella is pretendin' ta be a mommy so dey could join da mommy tournament. Dat means..."

"Exactly! They're going to attack—!"

"Dey wanna learn more 'bout bein' mommies! Dey were jus' pretendin' ta hate mommies, but they rilly ackshully wanna be mommies! Isso nice!"

"That…seems like an extreme misunderstanding… Is that why you didn't do anything?"

Trust in the goodness of everyone and the power of motherhood. That was Mamako for you.

Or rather, Child Mamako. "It's *really* hard to understand you…" She was only five years old now and didn't exactly have the best diction.

Child Mamako might have a heart as vast as the boundless ocean, but she wasn't always as implacable.

"But if dey wanna fights, den I'll give 'em a fights!"

"Whoa! Mamako's on fire!"

"Uh-huh! 'Cause, 'cause…dey washed Ma-kun's shirt sooo good! And it hurt so bad!"

She was sulking now.

"Mama's got her cheeks all puffed up! She's so angry!"

"That jealous energy's certainly putting her in overdrive…," noted Medhi.

"I really wish she'd stop that!"

"Mommy's never ever gonna lose where you're concerned, Ma-kun! 'Cause I'm your mommy! …So Mommy's gonna make a lunch that Ma-kun thinks is yummy and be your numba one mommy! Got dat, Ma-kun?"

"Yeah, yeah, sure. If you're all fired up, that's good! Let's do this!"

Those in the hall had fallen silent with surprise, but now they started cheering again.

The match was heating up. Sorente headed for the ingredients counter first and retrieved what they needed.

But their other opponent, the mysterious mother, Hahako, seemed to have stopped in her tracks.

Mamako was surrounded by Masato and the girls. But there was no one around the mysterious mother. Faced with a situation she couldn't copycat, she seemed at a loss…

No time to watch her now! We've got work to do!

It still bugged him, but first they had to win.

But then…

More trouble!

"Uh? Ma-kun! Oh no! Dis kitchen is HUUUGE!"

"It's not huge; you're just small! Did you not notice?"

"This calls for…Masato! Time to be her step stool!"

"We know how much you wanted a little kid to step on you."

"I have no idea what you mean, I'm not into that, you've got me all wrong, and however little she is, she's still my mom, so how could I ever take pleasure in that?"

"Oh, I found a stool! Use this!"

Party coordination solved that crisis.

Now Child Mamako could cook.

"'Kay, den Mommy's gonna do da cookin', and you guys go bring me what you wanna eat."

"It's too much for you to do alone," said Medhi. "Let me help—"

"As if! Porta, gimme a hand!" DEFENSE!

"R-right! I can help hold Medhi back!" DEFENSE!

"If Medhi cooks, the only thing we'll get is a Mysterious Object X! I'll leave her to you guys!"

Wise and Porta tackled the self-imposed trouble head-on, while Masato ran for the ingredients table.

Sorente was already there, gathering food. Masato took his place next to her.

"So just to get it out there… You're two of the Four Heavenly Kings, right?"

"Whaaaaaat?! I—I—I don't know what you could meeean!"

"You're using really specific skills, and you think you can keep hiding it? Don't be ridiculous."

"H-h-hide whaaaat?! We aren't hiding anythiiiing!"

"Even if our identities were revealed, and this just became a straight-up brawl… Not that I think I'd lose or anything, but… Mamako Oosuki's absurd powers would definitely put us through the wringer. So it seems safer to just keep fighting like this, following the tournament rules… Not that I should have to explain that," the lower of the two girls under the robe explained.

Everyone knew who they were, but if they wanted to keep the charade going, fine.

It is probably better to keep going like this. Better than starting a fight and messing up the tournament...

In which case:

"Fine. Then you're Sorente, and we'll beat you by the tournament rules. Which means I need ingredients! And you can't have a lunch box without *tamagoyaki*!" Masato reached out for the pile of eggs. One ingredient down!

...Nope. He couldn't lift the egg.

"Huh? This egg is insanely heavy... Ohhh! That debuff skill!"

Masato's strength was super-low at the moment. "Then byeeeee!" As promised, Masato was just getting in the way. Sorente finished gathering ingredients and left.

"My equipment's supposed to have a fifty percent chance of blocking status effects, but it sure never seems to work properly! ...Argh! I've just gotta make do!"

Masato grabbed the stupidly heavy egg with both hands, straining every muscle to move it. "Hngggggg!" Veins bulged on his face and arms, his entire body shaking.

At last, he made it back to Mamako—

—who was in trouble again!

"Oh, Ma-kun! Dis is bad!"

"I've got enough trouble of my own! What? What else is there?"

"Lookit dis!"

Child Mamako was holding a pair of cooking chopsticks.

When she held them upright, they bent. She couldn't grip anything this way! And she definitely wouldn't be able to scramble any eggs, either.

"Yo, what the heck? How is that possible?"

He couldn't even begin to imagine what could cause this.

So he yelled, "What's going on here?!" a little too loud, glaring at Kitchen B.

Sorente was busy cooking.

"Heh-heh-heh. That debuff skill even works on objects now! Not that I—"

"You don't need to explaaaain! Just get that onion peeeeeled!"

Amante always explained whatever they wanted her to. Such a useful enemy, really.

So that cleared that up.

"Damn! One after another... We've gotta do something!"

"But...what can we do?"

It wasn't just the chopsticks. The knife's edge was all round and couldn't cut much of anything. The ladle had holes in it. The rest of the kitchen equipment was equally useless. All Masato and Child Mamako could do was stare at each other, at a total loss.

But then...

"Don't worry! You have me!"

...Porta stopped forcing Medhi away from the counter and came dashing over.

"Porta... Oh, right! With Item Creation, we can make new tools! ...But wait, the skill's affecting you, too, so you might not manage..."

"Don't worry! I can do it!"

"...You're sure?"

"I am! When they made me a babysitter... I thought I could never do that, but when I tried anyway, I managed it somehow! This is the same thing! If I just try my best, I'm sure I can do it!"

Her eyes were shining with the purest light. Overflowing with belief in her potential—and the resolve to do whatever it took.

This made him want to trust her.

"Okay, then. Hook us up."

"Right! Leave it to me!"

Porta opened her shoulder bag and took out some wood and iron. She put the ingredients together and activated her skill!

"Will it be good? It'll be good! A good item...done!"

A burst of light appeared in Porta's arms, and when it died down...

...she'd made chopsticks, a knife, a frying pan, and a pot—everything they needed for making lunch. And they all were exactly the right size for Child Mamako to use. Perfect!

"Wow, great success! Well done!"

"Yes! I did it! ...Here, Mama! Make a delicious lunch, please!"

"Dat's such a big help! Tanks, Porta!"

Child Mamako took the tools and started cooking.

Meanwhile, in Kitchen B, Sorente was throwing a tantrum.

"Arghhhh! Mamako started cookiiiing! This suuuucks!"

"See? This is the power of friendship! This is our power!" Masato made Porta's success sound like his own, but no matter.

Mamako had the eggs scrambled, the pan on the stove, and was about to start frying when...

More trouble arrived!

"Oh? What's goin' on? Da burner won't light." *Click, click.*

"Crap! The burner's stats are debuffed, too!"

At this rate, they'd never get the *tamagoyaki* done. Or any other dishes. This was bad news.

Nah, just kidding. Masato had an idea.

"Heh... Certainly a surprising twist, but not a problem for us. After all...our party comes with our own personal fuel supply! Right, Wise?"

"I am *not* your fuel supply! At least call me a flamethrower or something! Geez!" Grumbling, Wise came running over.

She pulled out her magic tome and held out a hand toward the stove.

"I just need to light the fire with my magic, right? ...Honestly, this is gonna be rough..."

"Rough? ...Y-you don't mean...? Even though nobody's done anything to you, you've somehow managed to get your magic sealed again?! How useless can you get?!"

"I have not! That's not it! Just...my stats are really low, so I might not be able to use magic properly, okay?!"

"Oh, well... That makes sense. But you'll find a way to pull it off, right? You're the ultimate Sage."

He gave her a teasing poke in the shoulder.

Wise shot him a mischievous grin and kicked his shin in return.

"Ha-ha! Of course. Just you watch... *Spara la magia per mirare... Fuoco Fiamma!* And! *Fuoco Fiamma!*"

Wise chain cast. And flames danced in the burner, giving off a powerful heat…

…or rather, an extremely small flame appeared, like a single match.

"Wait, seriously?! That was my full power!!"

"Even discounting Wise being Wise, I guess there's nothing we can do to escape the debuff…"

"Do you have to be such a dick about it? And hold up! I'm not done yet! The way I am now…I can use the power of moms to overcome my limits! I think!"

"The power of moms…?"

Wise closed her eyes, concentrating.

"All the moms in this world can do, like, the most insane stuff, y'know? And with all the babysitting I've done, it's kinda like I've taken one step closer to motherhood… So I feel like I oughta be able to pull off something a little amazing myself!"

"You…really half-assed that, didn't you…?"

"Half-assed or not, keep your eyes peeled and watch! Here goes! …Hnggggg! …Stat debuffs…are *nothing* compared to babysittiiing!!"

For a fifteen-year-old girl, that was definitely an unprecedented burden.

Yet, along the way, she definitely felt the joy sparked by a child's touch, a joy that gave her the power to buck this sinister skill.

The tiny flames on the burner spread around the ring, becoming high heat!

"Whoa! You really did it! Wise, you're amazing!"

"Ha-ha! Of course I did it! I mean, I'm the ultimate Sage!"

"Oh, da fire's lit! Great! Wise, just keep it like dat, pwease!"

The pan went on the fire, oil in the pan, scrambled eggs poured in. The sound of the eggs sizzling already got their appetites going to an uncomfortable degree.

The audience members were watching Child Mamako cook, enraptured. You could almost hear their stomachs rumbling.

The only person complaining was the lower girl inside Sorente.

"Cooking over magic fire when the burner's busted? …The nerve!"

"Yeah? Yeah? See that? This is our power! Bwa-ha-ha!" Masato couldn't see her face under the robe, but he was sure it was oh so frustrated.

Feeling great about that, he started getting the next dish ready. What should it be?

"Next on the lunch menu... Right! Bacon-wrapped asparagus!"

A classic. A meat-and-veggie combo as tasty as it was healthy. Masato ran over to the ingredients counter, hunting for the asparagus...

...but found more trouble instead!

The asparagus provided was wilted. Maybe even withered!

"You've gotta be kidding! How...? Oh, is this Sorella's skill again?!"

She'd lowered the stats on the ingredients—including the vital freshness stat.

They were all done for. Every vegetable was dried out completely, turning brown and starting to disintegrate. The meat and fish were giving off a rotten stench. Not only was this stuff inedible, he could barely stand to look at it.

There's no way we can cook anything like this... Argh, what now?

He could go shopping and get more. That was the only idea he had, but then:

"It seems this is my chance to shine."

Medhi came walking slowly forward.

"Good timing, Medhi! We need a transport spell to—"

"No, there's no need for any shopping. We'll use these ingredients. As a consummate Cleric, I shall restore them with a recovery spell."

"A recovery spell? ...You can do that? It works on ingredients?"

Recovery spells in this world were your standard RPG spells, used to recover damage taken in combat or cure status effects.

They were only used on characters and shouldn't have any effect on physical objects...

But Medhi simply smiled her most beautiful smile and pointed her staff at the perishing ingredients.

"Porta and Wise aren't the only ones who've grown. I, too, learned a few small things from babysitting."

"Like...?"

"Perhaps I am still too inexperienced to put them into words... But I will say this. Mothers have a mystic—nay, miraculous power."

"Miraculous, huh...?"

"I sensed it myself. So observe. I, too, will bring about one or two minor miracles... *Spara la magia per mirare... Rianimato!*"

The staff released the light of life and poured it down on the dying ingredients.

A spell that should have had no effect...had an effect. The wilted vegetables were completely revitalized. The rotting meat and fish were no longer rotting. In the blink of an eye, all the ingredients were in perfect condition again.

"Wow! Medhi, you did it!"

"Yes! A much clearer success than Wise's extremely tiny boost to that flame!"

"You could've skipped the snide comment for once, but still... Well done! Magnificent! ...Okay, I'll just bring these to Mom."

With his strength reduced, the asparagus and bacon were incredibly heavy, but he managed to haul them over to Child Mamako.

As he did, he cast a sidelong glance at Sorente.

"Oh? Is someone being a sore loser? Oh yes! Right over there!"

"Arghhh... Who uses magic to restore ingredieeeents? That doesn't even make seeeense!"

"Causing miracles? Who do you think you are?!"

"Bwa-ha-ha! This is our true power! Yee-haw!"

Masato was getting carried away. Excessively so. He was in such a good mood, he actually started skipping... But then:

Trouble!

"Oh dear! Ma-kun, ovah here!"

"Right, this is it! It's my turn now! Time for me to show how all the hard work I've put into this hero thing has paid off!"

Masato ran to her side, ready for anything.

Child Mamako was holding a piece of the *tamagoyaki* in her chopsticks and glaring down at the lunch box on the counter.

"Mom! What's up? I'll solve whatever this problem is, so just lemme know how!"

"Well, dere's just one pwoblem."

Child Mamako put the *tamagoyaki* in the corner of the lunch box.

But the *tamagoyaki* inexplicably jumped up, flying out of the box.

"When I put it in like dis, it just pops wight back out! I dunno what ta do."

"Hmm, hmm… This is…probably Amante's doing. I bet she put her reflection skill on the lunch box so that every time you try to put something inside, it gets thrown back out. That must be it."

Pretty serious. At this rate, they'd never get the lunch assembled, and Child Mamako would lose.

But not to worry—Masato already had an idea how to handle things.

Masato picked up the lunch box lid and held it ready.

"Okay, Mom! Put that *tamagoyaki* back inside!"

"But…"

"Don't worry! I've got this! Trust in your son's power!"

"…Okie. Mommy twusts you, Ma-kun."

Mother and child stared into each other's eyes and nodded. "Here we go, Ma-kun!" Child Mamako placed the *tamagoyaki* inside the lunch box.

Immediately, Masato—

"Ohhhhh! How's this?!"

—let loose a passionate bellow, then slammed the lid of the box closed! And held it down!

"Nice! …Ungh, this is pretty tough!"

The pressure of the egg against the lid was incredible. If he eased off even a little, it would literally knock him off his feet. This was bad. He was in real danger.

But he wasn't giving in!

"You're messing with the wrong guy! This is my powerrrrrrrr! Rahhhhh!"

He put his full strength into it, fighting the *tamagoyaki* as it slammed against the inside of the lid, refusing to let it out.

Masato was in the fight of his life! His very life was on the line!

He was far too focused to notice anything around him! Even if he wasn't, he wouldn't have looked! No one look at him! No one speak to him!

"Er, um... M-Ma-kun? Calm down a li'l, okie?"

"Mamako, I know you're worried, but just leave him to it. He's gonna be fine," Wise reassured her. "Just ignore him and make the rest of the lunch."

"He has no choice but to get all worked up. Getting drunk on the idea of a battle... That's how he gets through his days," said Medhi. "The sheer effort brings a tear to my eyes."

"Masato can only get through his days if he's drunk... He's so grown up!" Porta gushed.

Pay no heed to the opponents, either!

"Uh, ummmm... I'm starting to feeeeel...sorry for hiiiim?"

"I feel like I've done something truly despicable. We should've come up with some other way! Something that allowed Masato to demonstrate his power the way his companions did. I'm sorry; I'm so sorry!"

He wasn't listening! He didn't hear a thing!

Back in the broadcast booth, Shiraaase grabbed the mic.

"Everyone, please. The hero may just be holding a lid on a lunch box, but let's give him a warm round of applause anyway."

"Stop! Stop being nice to me! Stop iiiiiiiiiiiiiiit!!"

Bathed in the warmth of the applause, the hero's tears flowed unceasing.

Everyone had left Masato sobbing in a heap.

Onstage, the results of the match were being judged.

The lunch box Child Mamako made was on the judge's table. Next to it was the lunch box Sorente had made. Both were accompanied by a generous helping of white rice.

Child Mamako's lunch was a mom lunch, filled with love: *tamagoyaki*, bacon-wrapped asparagus, spinach in sesame sauce, and cherry tomatoes.

Sorente's was surprisingly solid, too. They also went with *tamagoyaki*, alongside a meat-and-veggie stir-fry, buttered corn, *yakisoba*, and tangerines for dessert.

Both looked delicious.

"Lessee which of us deserves ta be Ma-kun's mommy!"

"You're waaaay too into thiiiiis, Mamakoooo."

"You get so pushy where your son's concerned… It's terrifying."

Child Mamako's aura was burning bright, her tiny finger pointed directly at Sorente. This girl was on FIRE!

She was so worked up, even her own party members were starting to shake their heads.

"H-hey, Mamako, take a breather. You can't make this fight all about them! You've still got one more opponent!"

They looked toward Kitchen C, where the mysterious mother, Hahako, continued to cook. She seemed one step away from completion.

"She still has time, so perhaps we should wait?"

"What do you think, Ms. Shiraaase?" Porta called out.

"Let's see…" Shiraaase thought about it. "We should probably start the judging when all the lunches are done, but Mamako and Sorente seem to have bad blood between them, so… What do you think? Shall we settle your feud first?"

"Yeah! Let's do dis!"

"Urrrgghh… F-fiiiiine! Let's goooo!"

"We'd never back down in a battle against a mother! That's a fact!"

"Both parties agree. That settles that! …Since it seems they are competing to see if Mamako or Sorente would be a better mother for Masato…"

"Waaaaaait! Only Mamako is hung up on thaaaaat!"

"We're not trying to be Masato Oosuki's mother at all! We just want to win!"

"I believe Masato would be the best judge of such a contest. We'll have Masato eat the lunches you made and decide which is his mother's. Do you agree?"

Child Mamako nodded. Suspicious mother Sorente reluctantly did the same. The crowd cheered in approval. Settled!

Masato's turn. "*Sniffle*… Huh? What?" "C'mon, Masato!" Wise dragged him to his feet. "Get ready!" Medhi placed a chair for him and sat him down on it. "I'll help, too!" Porta said, blindfolding him.

Masato's taste test.

"Er, um… Seriously? I've really gotta do this? No time to soothe my emotional traum—"

"Quit grumbling and open wide! First one's up!"

"No, wait—mph!"

The food in his mouth was soft, fluffy—a *tamagoyaki*.

Oh. That is good. Perfectly cooked. Nicely done. But…

No, not yet. He had to try the other one before he could be sure.

"Okay, Masato. Time for the next one. Here!"

"Right… Ah…"

Something landed in his mouth, and he chewed it. A similar texture to the first one. This was also *tamagoyaki*…

But the moment it touched his tongue, he knew.

Oh yeah. This one.

This was a flavor created by a skill that children knew better than the mothers themselves.

Not a special capital-*S* skill, but one any mother had—A Mother's Cooking.

It was really good.

"…Whew."

Masato swallowed the egg and took off the blindfold.

He looked at Child Mamako, who had her hands clasped together like she was praying.

"I sensed A Mother's Cooking from the second one. That's the one Mom made. I knew it right away."

He avoided her gaze and kept his tone curt.

"I knew you'd get it, Ma-kun! Mommy's so happy! Supa-happy! I've neva been so happy! Oh… What's happenin' ta Mommy now?!"

"Er, uh… Mom?! Whoa?!"

Child Mamako had suddenly begun to glow—and way beyond the usual A Mother's Light level. This luminosity exceeded well over the usual max threshold.

…And when the light subsided, she was no longer a child, but back in her usual body.

She immediately threw her arms around him. Mom's large boobs were right in his face, one on each side, squeezing…

"Ma-kun! Thank you! Thank you so much!" *Squeeze!*

"H-hey! Mmphhh!!"

"Oh, Mamako's back to normal!"

"That's it! The evil spell's gone!"

"Like something out of a fairy tale!"

"The prince saves the princess, but she turns out to be his own mom?! That's literally the most tragic fairy tale ever! The prince is ready to cry!"

It might be a tragedy for Prince Masato, but this story had a happy ending.

Masato had accepted Mamako as his mother. The unshakable bond between them proven, a wave of emotion surged through the crowd. "What a lovely story!" "I'm so jealous!" The mothers in the kid's area were all touched, clapping through tears.

Mamako had faced the suspicious mother, Sorente, and won. Her bonds with her son deepened, and she was guaranteed to reach the finals. And they lived happily ever...

At least, an ending like that would have been nice.

"Arghhh! This is ridiculouuuus! After we made her a chiiiild, she could still cook like a moooom! And she easily got her original form baaack! How is that poooossible?! ...That leaves us with no choiiice! ...Amanteee! Let's goooo!"

"Right on! Let's end this dumb charade and settle this directly!"

Sorente raised a hand in the air.

In it was a jewel of the darkest hue.

"Is that jewel... No?!"

"Mwa-ha-haaa! Exaaaactly! This is an item that lets us control NPCs at wiiiiill!"

"The other competitors, the audience, even the children! They'll all be our slaves, and all will attack Mamako Oosuki... Heh-heh-heh... And what then?"

"Tch! We can't let that happen!"

Masato ran forward, trying to grab the jewel, but he was too late.

It shone with a dark light that penetrated the minds of all who saw it...

And then.

*   *   *

"Are you children up to no good again? …Tut, tut!"

A stern voice. A hand on her hip. An index finger raised.

A brilliant, massive, black laser beam fired as she scolded.

It went from the stage toward the tunnel and the waiting room. "Huuuuh?!" "No way?!" It swallowed Sorente, the black light passing through them. And the dark jewel shattered.

And when the scold beam faded, Sorente was nowhere to be seen. Just the bare stage, with a half-pipe-shaped groove cut in it.

"Um… Wha—?"

Masato stared at the groove in the stage, forcing his mind to work.

That was a Tut, tut! *right?*

The color was different, but it was the same laser Mamako fired when she was really scolding someone.

But it wasn't Mamako who'd fired it—she was still standing next to Masato, looking every bit as stunned as he was.

It came from Kitchen C. And in Kitchen C was…

"……"

…the mysterious mother, Hahako.

Her expression was still as gloomy and unreadable as ever. She walked over to Masato…and held out a lunch box.

The lunch box contained *tamagoyaki*, bacon-wrapped asparagus, spinach in sesame sauce, and cherry tomatoes. The menu, placement, and quality were exactly like Mamako's lunch.

"Er… Uhhhh… You want me to eat this?"

Hahako nodded.

The scent of it was calling to him. Masato reached out his chopsticks, starting with a bite of the *tamagoyaki*.

Instantly, he sensed A Mother's Cooking.

"You're kidding… This is Mom's home cooking… But how…?"

"Well, I'm your mommy. I am Masato's mommy," she whispered.

The woman who looked exactly like Mamako gave him a warm, motherly smile.

CHILD MAMAKO

SKILLS

A MOMMY'S LIGHT

When she gets excited, her whole body glows. Since she's so small, you can easily pick her up and carry her.

"TUT, TUT!"

More adorable than threatening since it's a child doing the scolding, but she can still fire lasers, so watch out.

STRENGTHS

Many of her stats have been reduced, but she can make up for it with help from those around her. Her stat values improve based on the number of helpers and their abilities.

WEAKNESSES

Faced with a younger version of his actual mother, Masato's interactions with her are sometimes awkward. Additionally, it's harder for her to speak clearly in this form, so she struggles to communicate.

STATS

STATS

MATERNITY: 100 / COOKING: 70? / LAUNDRY: 70?
CLEANING: 70? / SHOPPING: 70? / COMBAT: 70?
MA-KUN: 100

SPECIAL   YOUTH: 150

Chapter 5 | I Don't Understand Those Feelings Now, but...Maybe Someday?

Between the self-destruct fireworks of one competitor and the disappearance/annihilation of another (technically two others), the semifinals were certainly a roller coaster.

However, the results spoke for themselves—having both made lunches with A Mother's Cooking, Mamako and Hahako were the victors.

Originally, the finals had been scheduled for that afternoon...but since the stage and building were in need of repairs, the finals were postponed to the next day. Currently...

"Where'd they go...?"

"Good question..."

...Mamako, Masato, and Porta were searching the deserted building.

Porta really shined at times like this. Masato was carrying her on his shoulders so she could get an even better view.

"Well, Porta? Any sign of Sorente or Hahako?"

"Hmmm... I don't see them anywhere! I don't think they're nearby."

"Okay... Sorente is whatever, but I definitely want to talk to Hahako..."

If their enemy had vanished, cool. But Hahako's mysteries were bugging him.

Her appearance, mannerisms, and skills were near-perfect copies of Mamako's... And she had gone so far as to call herself Masato's mother. He needed to find out what she meant by that.

Then:

"We're back!"

"Thanks for waiting."

The light of a transport spell appeared over their heads, and Wise and Medhi dropped down for a landing.

From that angle, he could see right up their skirts, but Masato pretended he hadn't. "Be grateful I'm such a gentleman." "Huh? Why?" "I don't get it, either…" The secrets of the girl in pale-blue panties and the one in pure-white panties were preserved. Anyway…

"Good work, guys. How'd it go?"

"I took a look around, trying to figure out what happened to Amante and Sorella, but they've vanished into thin air. If that scold beam took care of them, that'd be just fine by me, but…Amante, in particular, is pointlessly tough and fast, so I bet they're still around somewhere."

"I went searching for Hahako but was unable to find her. The moment the match ended, she left the hall and was nowhere to be found."

"Huh… Well, thanks anyway."

"The other mothers are searching as well! Did they find anything?" asked Porta.

"I'm not holding my breath at this point…," replied Masato. "Better to gather everyone together and talk it over. Shiraaase included."

"Talk it over—got it!" said Mamako.

Which meant…

The bath.

"Uh, why are we in the bath?"

They were at the public baths at the heart of Meema, the town where the World Matriarchal Arts Tournament was held.

To accommodate as many races as the tournament attracted, there were baths ranging from bucket-sized ones for fairies to a pool-like bath even the fifteen-foot-tall giants could relax in. There were over fifty different baths within the massive facility.

The party members were in one of these, a large all-inclusive indoor bath.

"Whew… The water's perfect."

"The bigger the bath, the better! I'm in heaven!"

"I can feel all the fatigue just washing away. So divine."

"Ooooh… Baths this big always make me want to swim!"

The slightly flushed islands formed by Mamako's breasts were so large and round, they looked extremely difficult to land on. Medhi's islands were impressive, as well. Porta's were age appropriate, and the way she kept her shoulder bag balanced on her head was a sight to behold.

Meanwhile, it was probably best to ignore Wise, who was keeping herself submerged, doing her best impression of an undersea volcano. Any comment might cause her to erupt.

Beyond them...

"I've never bathed with so many people!" "Oh, really? Our village is always like this." "I'm swimming!" "Blub, blub!" "Hey! No swimming in the baths!" "Aw, really?" "Well... If you're a mermaid, I suppose it's okay." "Fish soup!" "Hey! Don't be mean!" "*Sigh...* This feels so good that we might split apart..." "Now then, maybe time to tempt someone..." "Go on!" "Wow, you're really ripped!" "N-no...not at all..." "I wanna go play with Porta!" "Don't move around too much; you're making waves." "Wah! Mom got swept away!" "A life adrift on the currents isn't so bad."

The elf mother, beastkin mother, ninja mother, mermaid mother, vampire mother, spirit mother, devil mother, angel mother, dragonewt mother, martial arts mother, giant mother, fairy mother, and all their kids were in the bath, too, each mother bringing their impressive physique and a whole lot of commotion with them.

And Masato was there as well, staring at the surface of the water, trying not to look at all the flesh tones around him.

"Why...why does nobody care? I'm not a kid anymore, but no one's even batting an eye. You'd think I'd at least get an 'Eek!' or even a 'Get out!' like, normally speaking? But they all just accept it..."

The reason was obvious. After all...

Masato's secret title, Mixed Bath Creep Level 3, became Mixed Bath Creep Level 4!

With this title, it was now possible to bathe with other mothers! "I really need to get rid of this title..." However, titles were not available for exchange.

Anyway.

"Knowing when to give up is vital when dealing with moms. As is our tradition, we reveal our hearts and bodies in a naked strategy session... So if the person in charge could go ahead and explain?"

Masato asked, lacking the guts to do more than briefly glance in her direction.

"Sadly, I, too, was unable to grasp the particulars… However, I shall infooorm you of what little I could gather."

Shiraaase was sitting right in front of Masato. Wearing nothing at all. Even Masato's extremely brief glance had been enough to verify that she was sitting bolt upright, her torso well above the water's surface. "Submerge those things!" "As you were, then." As much as she enjoyed teasing him, this was serious.

"Let's begin with Hahako… *Hahako* is simply the name submitted when she entered the tournament, so we have no way of verifying if that is her real name."

"You don't? That isn't something you can check with admin rights?"

"For test players or ordinary NPCs, we have data stored and can easily investigate. But Hahako's data isn't saved anywhere."

Shiraaase looked at him emphatically, checking to see if he understood what that meant.

Masato thought for a moment.

"So… Hahako is neither a player nor an NPC?"

"Exactly. She was neither invited here nor created by a programmer. She simply exists in this world somehow… The circumstances of her spawning are similar to Amante's, but while we've been able to trace that girl's history, this is clearly something else entirely."

"Huh… Er, wait, you traced it back? You're getting somewhere on your Libere Rebellion investigation, then?"

"Oops. I may have let that slip… I shall infooorm you about that at a later occasion. The situation is rather…complicated."

Shiraaase gave Porta a sidelong glance. "Huh?" Porta looked confused, clearly unsure what that meant.

Shiraaase turned back to Masato.

"At present, our best theory is that Hahako is a character created independently by the game's main system. This is little more than a guess, however."

"Independently…?"

"You mean the system just…made her? It can do that?"

"The main system carries out a number of automated processes to make the world of this game as believable as the real world: weather control, seasonal plant growth—countless necessary operations, all handled and processed self-sufficiently. In other words, it had the permissions necessary to affect changes to this entire world..."

"And it's used those permissions to create a new person? Then...why use all that to make...Hahako?"

"I'm not sure this is the right way to put it, but...perhaps out of... admiration? The purpose of this game is to create adventures for parents and children. It is particularly rich in information about mothers' actions... And I hardly need to say who has been the most active in that department."

"Yeah, the most ridiculous of all is right here with us."

Masato glanced sideways. "Oh? Who?" Mamako asked vapidly, smiling. Seemed like she'd stopped listening the second they mentioned the word *system*.

He sighed.

"Take all the data on Mom...copy her appearance and skills...and you get Hahako."

The most famous mom in this world—and one so powerful her hero son was frequently depressed. A super-mom who overcame any situation with powers beyond the pale.

Including her excessive youth, beauty, and generous bosom.

If you were gonna copy someone, who better than Mamako?

It made sense that Hahako's appearance and skills were identical.

"There is still much we don't yet understand, but given her strong interest in mothers and the need to investigate further, we allowed her to participate in the tournament... And the fact that she prevented the two Heavenly Kings from doing any harm in the last match is certainly a very positive sign. At the least, we shouldn't consider her an enemy."

"I agree. She didn't seem like a bad person... Still..."

"I know. The last thing she said... If she genuinely believes you are her son, that is cause for very serious concern. After all—"

"Ma-kun already has a mommy—me! Mommy is his mommy!" Mamako proclaimed loudly, leaping to her feet. "Heyyy! Siddown!" His mother's butt was right in front of Masato's face... He felt a sudden urge to slap it but controlled himself.

Since the tournament began, other mothers had been trying to lure Masato away, making Mamako extremely jealous, leading to some very strange behavior… But the current situation was clearly different. She seemed far more desperate.

Hahako had clearly meant what she said.

And Mamako had taken that as a real threat to her motherhood.

In which case…I should probably say something.

He should say it out loud. As her son.

Masato pulled her arm, sitting her back down. Facing her as mother and son.

"…Mom, listen a second. There's something I want you to hear."

"O-okay. What is it?"

"When I ate the lunch she made, it tasted like a mother's home cooking."

"Ma-kun?! Don't say that! Your mommy is—!"

"I know! I know that, but…when I ran into her, and she let me sleep on her lap, I got the same feeling. I know she's not you, but…it was really confusing. Even so…"

To lose sight of who it was who placed absolute faith in him, loved him unconditionally, the one person in all the world who did…

That was inexcusable. It made him feel like a bad son.

There was only one way to make up for that:

Believe in what was plain as day.

"My mom is sitting right here in front of me."

Masato cast aside the shred of doubt within him, speaking with conviction.

Tears welled up in Mamako's eyes.

And a moment later, her boobs came rocketing toward him, smacking him in the face. Warm, soft breasts mercilessly pressed against him!

"Euuagghhhhhhhh!! My eeeeeeeeyes!!"

"Yes! Mommy's your mommy! I knew you understood, Ma-kun!"

"I do! Just lemme goooo!"

"Oh, thank goodness! I'm so glad you said so! Now I just have to make Hahako understand that in tomorrow's match! Mommy will do her best!"

"Roger that! Okay! We're on the same page! Now let go of meeee!"

This naked mom hug was rapidly eroding Masato's HP bar.

His party and the assembled mothers were all beaming with delight at such familial bliss... The kids mostly just looked confused, but whatever!

Shiraaase nodded, looking satisfied.

"Our original plan was to let Hahako act freely and observe what she does. However, if she perceives someone else's child as her own, we can't stand idly by. This game is all about the bonds between parent and child, and to ensure she does not become a threat, we need Mamako to guide her."

"Then, by putting Mamako up against her... Oh, wait, we're forgetting something important! There's still that pain-in-the-ass duo who might've made it out alive."

"Our plan for the two Heavenly Kings was to gang up on them... As impressive as your growth has been, can we ask you to beat the snot out of them the moment they show themselves?" asked Shiraaase.

The girls were not about to let that challenge pass.

"Hell yeah!" Wise shouted, utterly confident. "We could take those idiots down in our sleep!"

"There's no way we'd lose to them. This should be smooth sailing."

"We've got Wise, Medhi, and Masato, so we'll be just fine! ...But..."

"Porta? What's wrong?" asked Shiraaase.

"I'm more worried about Mama's match than the Four Heavenly Kings. If Mama fights a copy of Mama, that could get real scary."

"Don't worry! It'll be fine!" chirped the beastkin mother, Growlette. "We'll keep a close eye on the match for you. No matter what happens, we moms will take care of it! ...Right, Invi?"

"Yes... Mamako may have outdone us, but this is a chance to prove how impressive we all are in our own right. This match's safety is guaranteed. You can take this devil's word for it."

"And this elf's as well. I'll provide the protection of the Mother Forest!"

Chaliele's oath was followed by a chorus of other voices: "I'll give the mermaid's word!" "And I the dragonewt's!" "And the angels!"

"And the spirits!" "Vampires!" "Fairies too!" "Me too! The giants!"
"A-and martial arts…!" "And you've got the protection of a ninja!"
They could probably count on an android oath, too.

"Well? With all of us offering guarantees, you gotta buy it! This
offer's only good for today! Right, Ms. Shiraaase?"

"This isn't a home shopping program, but…very well. I'll accept
your offer. Thank you."

Mamako would be facing Hahako directly. Mothers of all races
would be backing Mamako while the rest of the party would be watching out for the Four Heavenly Kings.

So:

"Let's all put our best foot forward in tomorrow's match!"

""""""Yeah!"""""

The finals were tomorrow. Everyone was pumped. When Mamako
shouted, the girls, moms, children who'd long stopped paying attention…all stood up, raising their fists in the air!

…Except for one. "Oh, Masato? Not joining in?" "Just leave me
alone!" In a forest of mom-and-girl flesh, Masato was forced to stay
seated.

The next day arrived. The World Matriarchal Arts Tournament. The
final battle.

For the first time, the skies were overcast. Ominous clouds loomed
over the tournament hall.

Fortunately, the hall itself was still packed—not an empty seat in the
house, everyone into it, the crowd roaring even though the match had
yet to begin.

The mothers who'd participated were in the stands this time—
worried about what was to come. Their children must have picked up
on the tension, because they were all sitting quietly.

Almost time.

"…Here we go."

In the broadcast booth, Shiraaase turned on the mic.

"Thank you for waiting! We will now begin the final battle. Here
come our contestants!"

A thunderous roar erupted, and a fanfare written for just this moment began to play.

From the entrance tunnel came...

"All right! ...Ma-kun! Mommy's gonna do her best!"

...Mamako. Walking straight forward.

Following behind her was the mysterious mother, Hahako. So many questions still remained.

"......?"

When Hahako reached the stage, her hollow eyes looked around the arena.

She seemed to be searching for Masato, but he was nowhere to be found.

"Next up, we'll be deciding the contents of the match... The draw box, please!"

"Yes! Leave it to me!" Porta came out of the tunnel carrying the box and ran over to Mamako. "Here!"

"Thank you."

Mamako drew a slip of paper.

Was it cooking? Cleaning? Laundry? Or—?

Combat

When she saw the slip Mamako held up, Shiraaase gritted her teeth. "Of all things to pull here... I'm certainly not looking forward to this."

But she'd drawn what she'd drawn. Shiraaase had to announce it.

"The final round will be a trial of combat! To protect, to resist, and to follow through on one's beliefs, we must all fight. Mothers are no exception. Let us demonstrate the true power of a mother who means business. If the contestants could ready themselves..."

Onstage, Mamako was prepping for battle. "Mama, here!" "Thank you. You're always such a help!" Porta handed her Terra di Madre, the Holy Sword of Mother Earth, and Altura, the Holy Sword of Mother Ocean. Mamako equipped both swords, dual-wielding. She was ready. Porta quickly retreated.

Meanwhile...

"...Come."

…Hahako held out her hands, palms facing the floor.

Two swords rose out of the ground: one the color of flames, the other a deep blue.

Two Holy Swords very similar to the ones Mamako held.

Forcibly suppressing her surprise and anxiety, Shiraaase made the final announcement: "Then let's get this match started. Ready… Mom it!"

And with that, Shiraaase cut her mic, praying for Mamako's safety.

The rest was up to the two women onstage.

Mamako and Hahako faced each other, swords drawn.

"Do you mind if we chat a bit first?"

"…About what?"

"Ma-kun already has a mommy—that's me."

"*I* am Masato's true mother."

An attack delivered with a gentle smile, resisted with another. Neither smile wavered.

"Hmm… This is a pickle. I mean, Ma-kun is such a good boy, so I understand why you'd want to make him yours."

"That's not what this is. I am a mother, and therefore, Masato is my child."

"Because you're a mother, he's your child? …That's a strange way to put it."

"There's nothing strange about it. I'm a mother—the strongest mother. And as the strongest mother, my child is Masato."

"Um, pardon? That really doesn't make sense—"

But in response, Hahako swung Terra di Madre. The earth at their feet responded by shooting a large number of rock spikes out of the stage, aiming for Mamako.

Mamako swung her Terra di Madre at almost the same time, activating her own earth attack. The rock spikes struck one another.

Evenly matched in strength, the attacks canceled each other out.

Hahako lunged forward, attacking Mamako directly with Altura.

Mamako countered with Altura, too. The blue blades clashed.

Blades pressed together, each stared grimly into the other's face.

"Could you please listen to me for just a bit? That's not what makes someone Ma-kun's mommy. Strength has nothing to do with—"

"Masato's mother is the strongest. This information is correct. So...
If I defeat you, then I'll be the strongest, and I'll be Masato's mother."

Hahako suddenly retracted her sword and spun around.

Something whiplike came hurtling toward Mamako's face. Mamako quickly pulled back, dodging.

The whip...was a fluffy tail. Two tails—one red, one blue. Growing from Hahako's backside.

"Oh my! You have tails? Just like a beastkin!"

"You did, too. They were temporary, but you've been a beastkin yourself."

Hahako thrust her swords into the stage and charged toward Mamako.

She swung her hands, attacking with a beastkin's sharp claws. "Nng!" Mamako crossed her swords, blocking. The attack was repelled.

Hahako did an acrobatic backflip, grabbing her swords as she landed, before attacking again. Rock spikes and water bullets came in waves. "Hup!" Mamako quickly swung her swords, canceling the attacks in the nick of time.

"Y-you're amazing! Three attacks in a row! It was all I could do to defend—"

"I'm not done yet."

Hahako came slipping through the clashing spikes and bullets, closing the gap between them. She went directly into a spin, unleashing a two-hit tail attack.

Caught off guard, Mamako failed to block in time and was slapped on the cheek.

Fluffily.

"Goodness, that feels wonderful! Such bliss... But your attack hit me! That's pretty frustrating, come to think of it."

It had done no damage but was clearly a clean hit.

Without a chance to take a breath between attacks, the audience was left speechless.

In the broadcast booth, Porta and Shiraaase could barely believe their eyes.

"M-Mama took a hit... I've never seen that happen before..."

"We expected Hahako to be fairly strong, but...it's like they've taken

Mamako as a base and added other effective elements on top of that. And that isn't good."

Mamako was at a disadvantage. An unprecedented situation.

Yet, Mamako herself never wavered. Keeping a firm grip on her swords, she strode forward.

As a mother, this was a fight she couldn't lose.

"I am Ma-kun's mommy!"

"*I* am Masato's mother!"

And with these declarations, they clashed again, the battle for Masato growing fiercer still.

Meanwhile, Masato…

…was crouching behind the tournament hall, clutching his head.

"How many times are they gonna shout my name?! This is mortifying…!"

Their shouts were even louder than the roar of the crowd. Inescapable. "Ma-kun!" "Masato!" Both sounding just like Mamako, they screamed his name over and over. It was horrible.

But he couldn't let himself wallow in it.

"C'mon, Masato. Get the hell up. Let's go."

"We need to ensure the safety of the tournament hall. On your feet!"

"Y-yeah, I know."

Masato ran off after Wise and Medhi, doing his best not to hear the voices coming from inside the hall.

"Geez… You're always dragging your feet. What if Amante and Sorella did something while you were checked out?"

"If they're still alive, we need to search and destroy before they can do anything stupid."

"Uh, yeah… If they're gonna try something, we need to take them down so the match doesn't get— Wait. Uh… What the—?"

They were doing a circuit of the hall, and as the entrance came into view, Masato saw something:

A mob of people advancing down the large road leading to that entrance. All marching in step. And by people…

…he meant skeletons.

"Damn, an undead army!" cried Wise. "...That means—!"

"Sorella," Medhi cut in. "She's a necromancer, very good at making undead monsters do her bidding."

"Sadly, she's still alive and being a pain in our butts again! ...That's...a whole lot of enemies, and I'm already getting kinda depressed about it, but...let's do this!" Masato ran out into the street, and the three formed a line of defense.

Thanks to the staff in charge of traffic flow, all civilians had been evacuated. The army coming down the road like they owned the place included humanoid skeletons, zombies, and ghosts. Terrifying to look at, marching relentlessly forward...

...and from above, a flock of skeletal birds swooped down.

"...Wha—? Huh? Seriously?"

Masato blinked, checking again... Yep, he'd been right the first time. *Hell yeah! Flying enemies!*

"Right onnnn! Flying enemies are all MIIIINE!!"

The hero chosen by the sky would finally have a chance to unleash the full power of the Holy Sword of the Heavens!

Maybe this wasn't the time to revel in that, but he really almost never got a chance to do this!

Masato ran forward, grinning from ear to ear!

"Wise, Medhi! Back me up! I got the flying ones covered!"

"You dumbass! The heck are you thinking?! Do you even see the ones on the ground?!"

"Hurry and back him up! ...*Spara la magia per mirare... Purificare!*"

"Geez! Fine, I'll do it! ...*Spara la magia per mirare... Bomba Sfera!* And! *Bomba Sfera!*"

The approaching enemies were evaporated by holy light or blown away by explosions, clearing a path for Masato. "I love having reliable friends!" "You're getting chewed out later!" "And some fun corporal punishment with it!" "Please be gentle!!" He raced through the dust clouds left by defeated evil, taking a stand.

Then he held Firmamento high above and said a prayer.

Please... I just want to accomplish something. Just one thing!

Masato had been in Mamako's shadow for so long that he'd almost forgotten anything else was even possible.

And that wasn't all; in the third round, everyone else in the party had proven how much they'd grown. Porta's skills improved, Wise overcame her limits, and Medhi brought about a miracle.

But only Masato was left doing nothing... And that was unacceptable.

After all, he had feelings.

I don't always admit it, but...I want to do something for my mom, too!

Thoughts like this definitely made him cringe.

But in this moment, he meant it. Every part of him was on board with it.

"Skies above! Heavens! Swirling clouds! Come on! For once, understand how a son feels and gimme a little help, too! ...Right now, I just wanna blow the hell out of the enemies trying to get in my mom's waaaaay!"

With that yell, he swung the Holy Sword as hard as he could. A massive beam flew from the transparent blade, rising upward.

Nothing different about it, just like every attack he made... Or not.

The heavens answered him.

The beam flying upward split into four, each taking the form of a hawk.

"Whoa! What's happening?!"

"What the...? Masato's attack changed!"

"Has Masato awakened to a new power, too? That's absurd!"

"Yo, Medhi?! There's nothing absurd about it! You're so cruel!"

The beam hawks shot toward the enemy, attacking with sharp talons and beaks.

The bone birds crumbled instantly, their numbers dwindling in the blink of an eye.

"Are those Summons?! That seems like a really high-level power! I'm actually pissed now!"

"So am I. You have a lot of nerve! Unforgivable."

"My party's turned against me... But who cares?! Go! Get 'em, guys!"

He wiped away his tears, cheering his birds on.

And then:

! ...Something's coming?!

Trusting his instincts, Masato thrust his left arm forward, activating the function in his jacket to deploy a shield wall.

As he did, a tiger-striped blur crashed into him at inhuman speed, and a needlelike tip thrust forward, clashing with his shield and almost breaking through.

Amante had attacked him.

"Oh? You actually blocked that. That's a surprise."

"Yeah, it's a slow grind, but we're making progress... Hah!"

He swung, making her jump back and put a safe distance between them. "Figured you'd be here." "Time for payback!" Wise and Medhi joined him. Three against one...

Nope, three against two. Sorella was here as well—wearing gear covered in a skeleton-like pattern, riding on a magic tome the size of a tatami mat, floating languidly through the sky above.

"Yoo-hoooo! It's been aaaages!"

"No, it hasn't! We met yesterday, Sorente!"

"Whaaaaat?! Wh-who are you talking abouuuut?! I've never heard of themmmm!"

"The suspicious mother, Sorente, was actually us, but I don't—"

"Nah, you really don't need to explain that."

"Yes, we all knew the moment we first saw her."

""What? That's impossible!""

They were amazingly stupid, but that was irrelevant.

Masato's party members were here to fight.

"What were you planning on doing with that undead army?"

"Our infiltration scheme failed, so we've come to smash everything by force! But I don't need to explain that, do I?"

"Amante's habit of explaining these things is sooooo tiresome. But fiiiirst...there's something I want to aaaask. That other lady, the one who used 'Tut, tut!' just like Mamakoooo—who is sheeee? Mind filling us iiiiin?"

"Why would we? Don't be stupid. Wait... You already are."

"You'd better run away before we have to hurt you."

"Sheesh... It's obvious which of us is gonna get hurt here!"

"I thiiiink...you're all taking us far too liiiightly. Perhaps we should teach you the error of your waaaays."

Amante snorted, raising her rapier. Sorella got off her massive tome, gathering undead around her.

Masato's party versus two of the Heavenly Kings. Everyone glared. The slightest thing could set them all off...

Then.

"Er, what?"

"Hmm? Whaaaat?!"

Amante and Sorella both blinked, staring over the party's shoulders. Naturally, they weren't dumb enough to fall for such an obvious trick...in theory.

But then there was a loud noise, like an explosion. The ground beneath their feet shook.

What followed was a crackling sound like a tree growing really fast.

"Wh-what the...?" Masato couldn't stop himself from turning around.

Behind them, right by the tournament hall, a giant tree had fallen, taking part of the building with it.

"Yiiikes! That fight's getting pretty inteeeense! Isn't that an elf powerrrr?"

"I assumed Mamako Oosuki had this in the bag, but...could the worst have happened?"

"O-of course not! My mom would never let that... Ugh..."

Masato resisted the urge to dash off.

He couldn't just leave the two Heavenly Kings and go running into the hall...

"Masato! Go! We'll take care of these two!"

"We've leveled up! We can handle them. Go on!"

Wise and Medhi each gave him a push.

The two of them against the two Heavenly Kings was going to be a very hard battle. But...

But their eyes were serious. Telling him to trust his companions.

"Just to be clear...I'm not saying Mom is more important than you guys. Wise, Medhi, you're both important to me, too! Don't get the wrong idea!"

And with a *tsundere* cliché, Masato ran off as fast as he could.

As they watched him go, Wise sighed. "Geez... That idiot's always gotta say one thing too many."

"You look awfully happy about it, though. You've turned bright red, Wise."

"I have not! And you're looking pretty cheery yourself, Medhi!"

"Why wouldn't I? That was very nice… Anyway, enough girl talk."

They nodded and turned back to Amante and Sorella.

"You sure you wanna just let Masato run off?" Amante asked.

"We'll be fine. This is gonna be a super-fun girl's party. Who needs boys anyway?"

"Girls versus giiiiirls, crushing one another in seeecret."

"What a coincidence—I agree. You can never let people see any violence unfold."

"I feel like you let people see that all the time, Medhi, but whatever. Let's do this!"

Wise focused, raising her magic power. Amante pointed her rapier at her.

Medhi tightened her grip on her staff. Sorella opened the giant tome, her undead army forming rows.

All waited for the right moment to strike. And the first to attack… was Amante.

"I don't need to tell you this, but none of your attacks will work on me!" Amante snarled, walking slowly forward. "I can reflect all attacks, and Wise, the Sage, can't do a thing to me! Just you watch! Ha-ha!"

"Fine with me. Bring it! …*Spara la magia per mirare*…," Wise started her chant.

"You're gonna use magic? Useless!"

"No harm in trying! …*Bomba Sfera!*"

A sphere of explosive magic was released…but rather than hit Amante, it was reflected away.

And in that instant, Wise chain cast her second spell.

"And! *Reflessione!*"

A barrier that reflected magic appeared around Wise, reflecting the explosive sphere.

The sphere went back to Amante, and this time, it wasn't reflected, scoring a direct hit. "Huh?" She looked totally surprised for a moment before the explosion's wind hit her.

It did only a tiny amount of damage, but the magic definitely landed.

"Hell yeah! It worked! ...I've been wondering if you could reflect reflected magic...and you can't!"

"Tch! I had no idea a trick like that would work, but I'm not going to admit that! ...In that case—"

"Oh, no you don't! ...*Spara la magia per mirare... Lento!* And! *Reflessione!*"

Amante tried to charge but was hit with a spell that slowed her down. A lot.

"Argh!" "Ha!" Amante tried punching anyway but was easily dodged.

"Well? Your reflection skill and ridiculous stats aren't scary at all now! Now we just have to find out which'll run out first: your health or my magic!"

"You little... Hey, Sorella! Help me out! Use your skill to lower this Sage's abilities!"

"Wait, no, don't do that!!"

Amante had turned to Sorella for help...but Sorella had her hands full.

"I can't right noooow! I'm in trouuuuble! ...Auughhh! Auuugh! Aughhhhh!"

Sorella was activating her debuff skill over and over. She'd already stacked it ten times.

But despite the concentrated effect, Medhi was moving normally, easily swinging her staff and smashing the undead monsters with it.

"Wh-whyyyyy?! Why doesn't it woooork?! I've stacked it so hiiiigh! You shouldn't even be able to staaaand! Whyyyyy?!"

"Oh, you'd like to know why? Then let's discuss."

Medhi cracked a skeleton's skull, then stomped on it.

Black mist seemed to ooze from her entire body as she wore a sinister grin.

"I had a very strict upbringing. I was told to excel no matter what."

"Th-that sooounds...really haaaard."

"It sure was. I struggled a lot. But it also seeded this attitude inside of me. I must always be the best. And when my skills aren't enough...I'm not satisfied. I'm disappointed. And I'm furious."

"Th-theeen…because your skills are debuuuuuffed…you're really angryyyy?"

"I'm about to snap." *Click.*

"Eeeeeeeeek?! Did I just hear a switch fliiiip?!"

The more her skills were lowered, the more the frustration, gloom, and dark power rose within Medhi.

Her white robes were stained with that dark power, making her look like some sort of evil mistress.

Droves of the undead army took a knee before her. Recognizing Medhi as their mistress, they turned to face Sorella's forces.

"Gahhhhhhhhhh?! You've wrested control of my monsterrrrrs?! But this is my powerrrr! My precious powerrrr!"

"Clerics are healers of a holy order. For one of us to enslave the dead…is delightful!"

"Do you even know what holy meeeeans?! …A-Amanteeee! Over heeeeere! Stand between us so her attacks don't hit meeee!"

"I'm the one who needs backup! Argh!"

Amante ran over to Sorella, and she and the undead shored their defenses.

Meanwhile, Wise and Medhi joined forces and marshaled their undead, strengthening their attacks.

"Looks like we're not so evenly matched."

"Even? We're cruising to victory… Now, Wise."

"Got it! Here goes! With our power…!"

"We shall inflict pain on you that will make you curse your very existence!"

"Uh, no, we're just gonna beat them, like, in a normal way… A-anyway, let's go!"

This girls' night out had never been peaceful, and they were about to turn the dial up to eleven.

Back at the tournament hall, Masato stepped through what the fallen tree had left of the entrance and saw…

"No way… Mom's in trouble?!"

Onstage, Mamako was covered in dust and debris. She didn't appear to be at all injured, but her shoulders were heaving, her breath ragged. She looked exhausted.

Meanwhile, Hahako was increasingly abnormal: two tails, pointy elf ears, wings like a devil that lofted her into the air.

They both noticed Masato.

"Ma-kun! You came to cheer Mommy on!"

"Masato! You're here to cheer for me, aren't you?!"

Mamako and Hahako were swinging similar swords, exchanging rock spikes and water bullets, even as they ran toward Masato. "Hey! Wait!" he pleaded, but they did no such thing.

Each grabbed an arm, pulling Masato onto the stage.

"No, wait, listen! I can't be on this stage!"

"Oh, of course you can, Ma-kun! Mommy would be delighted to have you with me!" *Grin.*

"I've been looking everywhere for you! You should be with your mother." *Grin.*

"Not my point! The match is ongoing, and if I'm here—!"

"*Those two are fighting over which of them is your mother, Masato,*" came Shiraaase's voice over the loudspeaker. "*Your presence here will speed things along. Therefore, I approve.*"

Masato turned to argue, but he saw Porta next to Shiraaase, nodding desperately, and thought better of it.

They want me here... So my absence makes things worse?

If Mamako was at a disadvantage, she needed help from Masato, the source of her energy. Maybe that was their point.

Fortunately, the audience seemed to approve of Masato's participation, too. The two mothers both insisted they were his mother and were battling over a child... An entirely appropriate theme for a mom-off—and one that had the crowd pretty worked up.

Masato was the key to all that. What he did would decide the battle's outcome.

"Sucks to get stuck with such a major role all of a sudden... But I guess this is a hero son's destiny."

"Come, Ma-kun! Be with Mommy!" *Squeeze.*

"Come, Masato! I am your real mother!" *Squeeze.*

"Okay, got it. First, both of you—let go."

Once he was free…

…Masato immediately stood by Mamako's side.

Hahako looked astonished.

"Masato? That's not right! I'm your mother!"

"My mother's a human. She doesn't have a tail, or elf ears, or devil wings. She may have temporarily acquired each of those, but she doesn't normally have any of them."

"You like me better that way? Then, see, I'm your mother!"

Hahako eliminated all traces of other races, reverting to her original form.

Then she held out her hand, but Masato just shook his head.

"S-something still isn't right? …Oh, I know! Your mother is the strongest of all… I just have to prove that's me!" Hahako brandished her sword, pointing the tip at Mamako. "I am the strongest mother—Masato's mother. I joined this tournament to prove that… Beating you will be the proof."

"The strongest mother is Ma-kun's mother… You keep repeating that, and it's the strangest thing." Mamako wasn't even holding a sword.

"Mom…?"

"Oh? Abandoning the fight?"

"No. That's not it—I simply realized: This battle isn't going to be won with swords. So I gave the swords a break. I always get so carried away when it comes to Ma-kun. And I know I've got to stop doing that. Mommy's mistake!" Mamako gently bonked herself on the head.

Then, smiling peacefully, she looked directly at Hahako.

"Everything Ma-kun and the others were talking about in the bath was too complicated for me, but I did understand one thing. You're someone who wants to become a mother."

"…………!"

This really seemed to rattle Hahako.

"And that's a truly wonderful feeling! I think you should be proud of that desire. But…I also think you don't really understand what a mother is."

"Then what…?"

"Being a mother means… Well, see?"

Mamako reached into her dress and pulled out a slim book from her bosom.

The cover read MATERNAL AND CHILD HEALTH (MCH) HAND-BOOK. "Wait, where were you keeping that?!" "It's important! I never go anywhere without it!" Masato's reaction aside, his mother's body had kept the handbook warm.

"This is proof of motherhood. And proof of a child. It has detailed records of everything from the moment the child was born until they grow up. How tall they were, how much they weighed, medical reports from when they got sick... Happy or sad, all sorts of memories get written down here."

"Memories..."

"Yes. These are my memories of Ma-kun. Proof we're mother and son."

"Proof... But I..."

Hahako reached into her bosom, searching... But no handbook emerged. She didn't have one.

"Of course, that's not everything. There are plenty of people not related by blood who fortune brought together that formed a wonderful parent-child relationship. However... And I do hate to be harsh, but let me make one thing very clear."

"Wait... Please! Wait! I...!"

"Without anything built between yourself and a child...you aren't a mother at all."

Mamako looked very apologetic but forced herself to tell the truth anyway.

The impact was immediate.

A creaking sound came from Hahako's heart as it ruptured.

Fissures ran across her face, neck, chest, sides, legs—her entire body.

"No... No, no, no! No! NOOO!"

"Um... Just calm down a moment..."

"Wait, Mom! Stay back! This looks dangerous!"

Masato leaped forward, putting Mamako behind him, and raised his sword.

Something emerged from inside Hahako. Crawling out from between the fissures were...hands, with the translucent beauty of noo-dlefish. But the way they moved—horrifying.

"I *am* a mother! I am! I'm the strongest mother in the world! ...I have a child... A child... My child!"

Tears running down her face, she looked at Masato and Mamako, then at the handbook. Fear in her eyes.

Then Hahako turned to the stands—the stands filled with children of audience members, children of the other tournament contestants... and Porta.

"Oh... There you are! Eh-hee-hee! Now then, come to your mother!"

Countless hands reached out from all over Hahako, touching children in the stands.

They were adorable children. It would never do to be rough with them. The hands just lightly brushed their heads.

Nothing more.

"Oh, Mom's calling me... Bye, Auntie! Bye-bye!"

"What are you saying?! *I'm* your mother! You know that, don't you?!"

"Mommy!" "I'm coming, Mommy!" "Let go!" "Lemme go!" "Wah!"

"Hey, wait! Where are you going?! Mommy's right here!"

Nothing seemed to have changed at all—but suddenly all the children thought Hahako was their mother. Their real mothers were desperately clinging to them, but some children got away.

Even Porta was affected. She quietly took the white hand in front of her and tried to follow it out of the broadcast booth.

"Ms. Shiraaase! I'm off to see my mom!"

"Wait! Snap out of it! You can't go!" An unexpected note of desperation in her voice, Shiraaase threw her arms around Porta, holding her back.

That was certainly surprising, but...Masato couldn't dwell on it.

"Ma-kun!"

"Yeah, I know! We gotta do something about these hands!"

Masato and Mamako attacked in tandem. His beam attacks and her rock spikes and water bullets began cutting down all the hands as they started to reach farther, extending outside the tournament hall.

But the severed hands quickly regrew. An endless supply, their numbers only increased.

And then the crowd turned ugly.

"What is wrong with you?! These are *our* children!"

"Only an idiot would try to steal children when their mothers are watching! You must be punished!"

"Y-you will learn the power of a mother who means business!"

The beastkin mother, Growlette; the dragonewt mother, Sammo Hung; the martial arts mother, Katou. The combat mothers leaped down onto the stage, attacking Hahako.

But...

"I'm a mother, and I mean business, too! I'm not going to lose here!"

"Don't be ridicu— Wah!"

As Growlette tried to slash with her claws, a number of white hands appeared around her, each taking Growlette's form and attacking at once. "Unh?!" With full beastkin power, she was slammed to the stage.

"This thing's something else! So that means... Katou, we need to attack together!"

"R-right! Hyaaah!"

"It doesn't matter how many of you there are. I'm the strongest mother. I can't be defeated."

Hahako caught both the dragon-breath attack and the mother's iron fist with her white hands.

Then...

"Sorry to come at you from behind! But you need to cool your head a little!"

"Angels aren't known for sneak attacks, but this is no time for principles!"

"Oh, but this is exactly what I'm into! I mean, I'm a devil! Hahhh!"

From Hahako's rear: the mermaid mother, Nakasao, with a water cannon. From the left: the angel mother, Mamariel, with a holy spear. From the right: the devil mother, Invi, with a slashing scythe.

And...

"Even I get pissed when you mess with my kid! Raaah!"

...the giant mother, Kaide. Her hands clasped together, she dropped a giant hammer on Hahako's head.

Concentrated attacks from five different directions!

"It's all useless—I am the strongest mother."

Hahako's white hands easily blocked all the attacks, captured the mothers, and slammed them into the ground and walls.

She was too powerful. Masato gritted his teeth.

"Damn! She really is as strong as she is awful! This is really bad!"

"I'm worried about the mothers! We need to tend to their wounds—and quickly!"

"Yeah, I'd love to… But the only person who can use recovery items or magic is…"

The other mothers were scattered through the stands, desperately trying to prevent their children from being stolen. They knew what was going on but weren't in any position to come to the rescue.

The party usually relied on Porta, but she'd been brainwashed, too.

Damn! If only Wise and Medhi were here!

Masato really wished they were. And as the thought crossed his mind…

"…Whaaaaaaaa—?!"

"…Eeeeeeeeeeeeeeek?!"

"Mm? Whoa!!"

…Heaven heard him. Wise and Medhi came tumbling from the sky above. Admittedly, wrapped in white hands.

When he cut those arms, they were all "Hah!" "Humph!" "Bwa?!" Masato made an excellent shock absorber, and they landed beautifully on him.

"So I'm not okay, but I guess the two of you are?!"

"We are! But what the heck?! What just grabbed us?!"

"The moment those things touched us, it was like our mothers calling our names! So bizarre! What are these hands?!"

"They're really dangerous! Anyway, I'm so glad you two are—"

"Gaaaaah?!" "Waaaahhhhh!"

"There's more coming?! Wait, that's…"

Amante and Sorella. Like the others, they were dragged in by the white hands.

In midair, Amante forcibly ripped the hands off them and hoisted Sorella onto her shoulders. "Masato Oosuki! Stay right there!" "Hell no! Go awa—mmph?!" Masato made an excellent shock absorber, and they landed beautifully on him as well.

"Hey! Why are you two here?!"

"Oh, shut up! It wasn't voluntary!"

"B-buuuut… My moooom… M-my moooom…was caaaalling…"

"Sorella! Get a grip! Coming when your mom calls you?! We're against moms! If moms— Augh, what are these creepy hands?!"

Mid-rant, Amante's eyes had landed on what was left of Hahako—no signs of her original form remained, just a mass of countless, writhing hands.

"U-um, Masato Oosuki… What is that?"

"The one you were worried about. She's capturing children, making them her kids, and trying to become a mother. Not that I need to explain that to you!"

"Yet, you just did. You're an idiot, Masato Oosuki."

"You're the last person who should say that!"

"But in that case… Sorella, let's retreat!"

"Yeaaaah… I don't want to be turned into a chiiiild… And she looks hard to beeeat… Let Masato's group handle herrr. Which meaaaaans… Bye-byeeee!"

Amante and Sorella hopped on the giant magic tome and flew away.

"Tch! They ran off!" groaned Masato.

"And just when we were about to finish them off after taking down their monster army! …Whatever! No time to mess with the Four Heavenly Kings now!"

"I've got the general idea, here! Wise and I will heal the wounded and draw the hands away! There's no time to waste!"

"Yeah! Go for it!"

"Please! And take care!"

Wise and Medhi ran off. Having reliable companions was a magnificent thing.

"Right… Mom, let's go."

"Yes! Let's!"

Masato and Mamako went after Hahako's main form.

A sad mass of desire, so desperate to be a mother that it was blindly reaching out in all directions.

Masato lowered his sword, putting it back in the scabbard.

"She's going about this all wrong… But in her own way, she's just desperate to be a mother. I feel like defeating her by attacking it isn't the right thing to do."

"You're right. We shouldn't be defeating her. We have to show her what being a mother and son is really about. Which means..."

Mamako smiled and showed him the MCH handbook.

What was a son supposed to do with that? Masato was totally lost... But lacking other options, he reached out and touched it. And then... "Whoa..." "Oh my!" ...The handbook began glowing and slowly floated upward.

This light hovered before them, growing longer and curving gently, like a saber—then it split in two.

Two swords appeared, the hilts joined by a ribbon.

Like an umbilical cord connecting the parent sword to its child.

"Are these...?"

"I'm not sure, but...I believe something wonderful is happening."

"Huh... I dunno... I'm getting exactly the opposite vibe..."

"We should use them!" Mamako reached out and grabbed the hilt in front of her. "Oh my! What a lovely sensation. It feels so right in my hand!"

"You just grab it without any hesitation at all. Geez, Mom... Fine. Let's just pretend these are some legendary swords, and..."

Nervous, Masato reached for the sword...

"Don't worry! Mommy will handle this!" *Snatch!*

"Huh? ...Waaaaaaaaaaaait!!"

Mamako grabbed the sword hovering in front of Masato, too. Dual-wielding, like always. "I just feel better with two swords!" "Heeeeeeeeeeeeey!!" Her son's screams fell on deaf ears.

Swords in both hands, Mamako glared at the thing Hahako had become.

"With these swords, I know I can do this! Our mother-son memories will reach you! This is Mommy and Ma-kun's memorial... Um... Memorial... *Hyah!*"

Mamako spontaneously acquired an ultimate attack.

The name—like she said, "Mommy and Ma-kun's Memorial Hyah!"

Mamako swung the sword in her right hand—Genitore, the parent blade. A warm wave spread out around her in all directions.

Memories of their time together reached Hahako—and anyone else the wave touched.

"Wah! Wahhh!"

"My, my! Aren't you a lively one!...Thank you. Thank you for being born."

Lying on a hospital bed, looking just as young as she did today, was Mamako, rubbing newborn Masato to her cheek.

"...Mm... Mm..."

"Drink lots and lots of Mommy's breast milk and get big and strong! Hee-hee."

In the living room at home, Mamako smiled as baby Masato breastfed.

"Nngh... Mmm... Mm!"

"That's it! Ma-kun, go on! Oh, look at how good you're walking! So good!"

Masato was holding himself up, and he took a step forward. His first step! Mamako was equipped with a *happi* coat and headband to cheer him on, beside herself with joy!

Each scene was an illusion brought to life by Genitore.

But each was a day that had really happened. A memorial of their time together.

Then Mamako swung the blade in her left hand—Figlio, the child blade. Another wave went out, adding more memories of their time together.

"Mommy! A big doggy! Big doggy! Wah!"

"There, there. Don't cry! Mommy's right here."

Masato was old enough to go out now, and they'd run into a Doberman on a walk. Scared, Masato started crying and threw his arms around Mamako's leg.

He was only a kid, so you couldn't blame him, but...it was still a little pathetic.

*　　*　　*

"Nuh-uh! I don't wanna! Wahhhhhhh!"

"If you don't go to the dentist, your toothache won't get better! Okay, Ma-kun?"

The moment he'd realized they were going to the dentist, Masato had thrown a tantrum. Mamako wasn't sure what to do, but he didn't care. He just decided to lie down on the sidewalk, kicking his legs, crying and screaming.

He was only a kid, but seriously, that was maybe a bit too childish.

"So, um, da pwesent I want is…is Mommy!"

"You want Mommy? Then Mommy's all yours, Ma-kun!"

Masato's fifth birthday party. His present was Mommy. Mamako gave him a big hug, and Masato kissed her on the cheek. He loved Mommy!

Asking for Mommy as a present was quite something! So innocent! Kids!

These scenes were shared with everyone.

"STOPPPPPP!! Please, no mooooooooore!! Don't show people something this embarrassiiiiiiiiiiiiiiing!! …Augh, it's too much… *Sob…*"

Masato immediately let out a bloodcurdling scream, but everyone ignored him.

Their family memories caused a change.

The bewitched children snapped back to their senses and went running to their real mothers. "Mommy!" "Geez! You scared me!" Their mothers held them close, scolding them but weeping tears of joy and relief. So beautiful.

Porta was back to normal, too.

"Um… Why are you hugging me, Ms. Shiraaase?"

"Good question… Do you mind if we stay like this a little longer?"

"Okay! Go ahead!"

Even those who weren't mother and child felt the need to fill the hole left in their hearts. Shiraaase had Porta sitting on her knees, arms tight around her.

The white hands filling the hall were vanishing one by one, washed away by the warm wave. Wise and Medhi breathed sighs of relief.

"Whew... Looks like that's that."

"It seems so. We shall have to discuss these memories with Masato in *great* detail later... But first, I need a rest."

"You seriously have the *best* personality."

The girls had endured two big fights in a row: the Four Heavenly Kings and whatever this was. Drained of MP and energy, they slumped to the ground, back-to-back, letting the fatigue wash over them.

When they glanced up, they noticed the skies had cleared, the oppressive clouds giving way to sunbeams.

Filled with a sudden urge to do laundry, Mamako let out a sigh.

"...Now, then."

She tucked the MCH handbook—now back in its original condition—between her breasts and turned to Hahako.

No longer a mass of writhing white, Hahako was in human form once more. The flood of pale hands was gone, as were the cracks on her skin.

Her face was buried in her hands. She was crying.

"Being the strongest doesn't make you a mother... Giving birth, raising them, making memories—*these* things make you a mother... B-but I have none of those... I was never a mother at all..."

"That's right. You weren't a mother. But..."

Mamako gave Hahako a warm embrace.

"You will be a wonderful mother. I mean, you want to be a mother so badly! I'm sure you'll be one someday."

"I...I will. Someday...I definitely will..."

"Yes! Become a mother! Let's mom together! Hee-hee!"

Hahako nodded several times in response to this encouragement.

A beautiful smile on her tearstained face, Hahako's body slowly faded away. She was gone.

Seeing this, Shiraaase switched her mic back on.

"And that's the match! The winner of the World Matriarchal Arts Tournament is Mamako Oosuki!"

"Huh? Winner? ...Oh, that's right! This was the finals! My head got so full of Ma-kun, I totally forgot! I'm such a ditzy mommy! Hee-hee!"

Mamako may have only just remembered...

...but the crowd was cheering her victory, their applause mingled with laughter.

MAMAKO OOSUKI

SKILLS

A MOTHER'S LIGHT
When she gets excited, her whole body glows. Controlling this light is not one of her strong suits.

"TUT, TUT!"
When she scolds someone, she fires a laser beam. Since it's just a scolding, it doesn't count as an attack but is nonetheless extremely destructive.

STRENGTHS

Pretty much an all-powerful mom. Highly skilled with anything related to housework or Masato.

WEAKNESSES

A little too focused on Masato, which tends to distract her. A careless word from him can render her totally helpless.

STATS

STATS

MATERNITY: 100 / COOKING: 100 / LAUNDRY: 100
CLEANING: 100 / SHOPPING: 100 / COMBAT: 100
MA-KUN: 100

SPECIAL ENTHUSIASM: 100

Epilogue

The final round of the World Matriarchal Arts Tournament was over.

Tonight was a festival. The passion of the day's events had yet to dissipate, and the streets of Meema were packed. Elves and beastkin playing music, angels and devils singing, tiny fairies and giants dancing hand in hand. All sorts of races from all over the world partying the day away.

Her back to the town...

"..."

...Hahako wandered aimlessly through a grassy field.

Where should she go? She didn't know.

But she knew what she had to do.

"I will become a mother... And to do that...I need a child."

Hahako walked on, longing for the moment when her child would be in her arms.

Meanwhile, in a forest far from Meema:

Amante and Sorella were standing before a dark vortex hovering in the shadows, looking unsure of themselves.

"...Guess we just keep an eye on her? That all we're gonna do about Hahako?"

"It seems like she wants to be a motherrrr... So why not leave her to iiiiit?"

A third voice came from the vortex—an uncanny voice. Nothing about it was clear, not even the speaker's gender.

"As long as it remains a mere desire on her part, you may ignore her." The voice paused, as if considering things. *"However, if there is any*

chance she could harm Porta, take her down immediately. Prioritize her over Mamako Oosuki."

There was a hint of anger in the voice. Orders given, the vortex vanished.

Once they were sure all traces of it were gone, Amante and Sorella began whispering to each other.

"...Porta, huh?"

"Our master is definitely fixated on herrrr. Lord only knows whyyy..."

"There's definitely something there. Like the master is Porta's..."

...family...or something...?

Amante shook off that thought and started walking.

"No point speculating. Our duty is to eliminate mothers and secure Porta. The Four Heavenly Kings see their missions through."

"Riiiiight. Don't want to make the master angryyyy... But what nee-ext? Find another Heavenly King and boost our foooorces?"

"Not a huge fan of that idea, but it's certainly an option... Let's move."

Amante and Sorella vanished into the dark depths of the forest, their matching black coats flapping.

Back in Meema:

The tournament hall itself had been repurposed as the main stage of the after-party. The kid's area was filled with stalls, different performers were doing shows in the stands, and the place was packed with people of all races.

But the more people gathered in any one place, the more problems arose. Like lost children.

But don't worry. This place has excellent babysitters.

"Mamaaaa! Where's my mamaaaa?! Wahhhhhh!"

"Argh, will you stop crying? I'll help you look, okay?"

"Excuse me, everyone! Is the mother of this human child nearby?"

"Oh! There's someone waving over there! I'm sure she's the mother!"

Originally, they'd been volunteer staff, but now...they were just volunteering. Wise, Medhi, and Porta were walking around the hall of their own accord, helping lost children. For as much as they'd resented helping the kids earlier, they certainly seemed to be having a good time.

And up onstage, an event was taking place.

"We're about to begin the WMC—the World Masato Championship!"

"Somebody make them stoppppp!"

Mic in hand, Shiraaase was standing by a chair, to which Masato was securely strapped.

"Hey! This isn't funny! We can't be doing this! We've gotta find out what happened to Hahako…!"

"After she disappeared, she re-formed outside of town. Don't worry… She's driven by the desire to become a mother. That usually isn't a bad thing. Just in case, we've upped our monitoring of her. If anything happens, we can swiftly deal with it."

"Y-yeah? Well, that's good, I guess…"

"So please enjoy the fun… Hahako has admitted she isn't a mother, which disqualifies her from the tournament… But nevertheless, Mamako's victory is undeniable. Celebrate it with her!"

"I'm all for celebrating, but that has nothing to do with the current situation!"

"Well then, everyone looking to score points with Masato, please join us onstage! Volunteer or be volunteered! No method is off-limits! Come one, come all!"

"Stop trying to make this happen! Score?! What does that even mean?! …Aughhhh!"

Mothers from the tournament were streaming onto the stage. He was soon surrounded by moms of all races. This was really happening. At last…

He had a harem!

"Look, Masato! Elf-mom ears!" *Twitch, twitch.* "How's my tail for ya?" *Fluff, fluff.* "A *shishamo* mermaid!" Such glittery scales! ☆ "Eat some *mapo doufu*, and you can breathe fire!" Dragon fire! "Time to get those teeth brushed!" Vampire Mom went *swish, swish*! "D-do you like Mommy's six-pack?" *Flexxx!* "Oh, a pocket just for me!" The tiny fairy mother squirmed about! "Is that Mommy making your heart pound? You nauuughty boy!" An overly sultry devil! "Time to fuse!" Fire, water, earth, and wind performed spirit fusion with their son! "Time for your enhancement operation!" Was Masato finally becoming an android?! "Want to join me in Heaven?" The angel had come for him! "Yay! I wanna join in!" The giant mother picked him up. "Time for some ninja arts! Nin!" Her ninja scroll became a sushi roll! ...Wait, that was just normal sleight of hand.

Masato was pulled this way and that, lots of skin contact, lots of feels copped! This was...

...way too much, honestly!

"Listen, I'm absolutely flattered, but hang on!! I really don't think I'm equipped for a harem of moms! ...Huh?"

Suddenly, he realized he was no longer tied to the chair. He was free. Someone had untied him.

Chaliele and Growlette, representing all the moms gathered, both smiled kindly at Masato.

"I hoped to capture your heart and make you my child," the elf mother said. "But..."

"But after seeing those memories?" the beastkin mother chimed in. "We all know whose kid you are."

"Uh, yeah... Right."

"So go on. Go to Mamako."

"I think she's in the waiting room. Go congratulate her on her victory."

"Good point. I still haven't told her... Bye, then!"

They gave him a push, and he leaped off the stage.

Just then, he bumped into the girls.

"Okay, Masato! This is your last battle! Show us how much you've grown!"

"How will Masato fare against his own mother, Mamako? This will be a fierce battle indeed."

"Good luck! I'll be cheering my hardest for you!"

"Guys, I'm not gonna fight her... Well anyway, here I go!"

Each of them gave him a pat on his back, and he was off.

Masato raced through the tunnel into the waiting room.

Mamako...was sitting on a bench in the corner, flipping through a photo album.

"Hey, Mom! Is that the prize?"

"Oh, Ma-kun! Yes, it is. It's lovely! ...See, look!"

Mamako showed him the tournament grand prize, the Mother-Child

Album. It looked like any other photo album, but the pages were filled with auto-captured images of their time together here.

Animal Mamako, Elf Mamako, Devil Mamako, Child Mamako. Images of all Mamako's transformations, and next to them—Masato's exaggerated, snot-spewing reactions. "Yeah, don't show me those." Masato closed the album.

Now was the time for the hero son to test his mettle.

"Uh, Mom. I didn't say this properly, so let me say it now... Congratulations on your victory."

Simple, to the point. What he should be saying.

But Mamako had her head down, looking unhappy.

"Mom...?"

"Thank you. I'm always happy to get praise from you, Ma-kun... But... *Sigh...*"

"Wow, it's not like you to sigh. What's the matter? ...Oh, I know... This is about Hahako, right?"

"Well, yes, but that's not all... Ma-kun, listen."

Mamako got up on her knees on the bench, patting the space in front of her. She wanted Masato to sit there, apparently. She looked awfully serious. "Wh-what?" This sounded important. He did as she asked, sitting on his knees facing her.

And then her cheeks puffed up.

"Ma-kun! Mommy's hopping mad!"

"Wh-why are you mad?! Or rather, sulking?!"

"I was watching, you know! I saw those other mothers pulling you around! I could tell it was going to your head! You were loving it, you cheater!"

"So that's what was bugging you! And that's not cheating!"

"You like other moms more than your own mommy..." She sniffed.

"And now you're gonna cry? No, wait, calm down! Of course I don't! I've only got one mom, and she's right in front of me!"

"...You mean it?"

"Of course! I swear! I swear on our memories together!"

"On our memories? Then...will you give Mommy a kiss like you used to?"

"Huh? Where'd that come from?! You're acting weird!"

Each time Mamako got jealous, it activated one of her special skills, A Mother's Envy.

This skill could store up energy over time, and Masato's cheating had driven it past the critical point, forcing her to make an outrageous demand! Her cheek turned toward Masato, urging him to seal his vow with a kiss!

A boy his age kissing his mother's cheek? This was a tougher battle than facing a million monsters at once.

Argh... But if that settles things...I'd better just get it over with.

They were mother and son. It was fine. There was nothing weird about it! Kids kissed their moms all the time!

He took a quick look around, making sure there was no one there.

And then the hero son summoned all his courage!

...Smooch.

He planted a superfast kiss on Mamako's cheek.

"Th-that good enough? You satisfied now?!"

"Yes! Mommy is ever so happy! Hee-hee!" *GLOWWWW!*

"Yeah, yeah, okay! Too bright! Can't see!"

Mamako was far too happy and glowing way too brilliantly. Getting a kiss from her son was a much greater source of joy than winning the tournament. She was so incredibly happy, she didn't know what to do with herself.

And seeing her like this made him feel a little bit like it might have been worth it...

...at least until ten seconds later, when he spotted the rest of the party watching and then promptly freaked out.

Afterword

Hello, everyone. This is Inaka.

Thanks to the support of readers in Japan and abroad, Volume 5 is now on sale. I'm very grateful.

I never imagined *Mom* would go overseas! In February 2018, I even did an autograph event thanks to the generosity of Kadokawa Taiwan. It was amazing.

I'd like to thank everyone I met in Taiwan and all the readers there. I also wish to express my condolences to anyone affected by the earthquake that happened on February 6.

It feels like no time at all, but a year has passed since I set out on this adventure to answer the question *What is a mom light novel?* I am constantly groping in the dark, but I've received support from so many and thus continue to make my way forward.

Iida Pochi., my editor K, Meicha, who draws the manga, and everyone with publication and sales—thank you.

Ai Kayano did the honor of reading my book out loud. You can find it through the audiobook sales service Audible; so if you're curious, please have a listen.

In Japan and elsewhere, there are many plans afoot, and *Mom* will continue to grow. I sincerely hope this is only the beginning of a long relationship.

Finally:

This volume is full of many different moms, but there's one very unique mother close to me personally.

The kind of mom who plays big console titles like P5 and DQ11 in real time, competes with her junior-high-school-aged son in hunts in MHW, gets addicted to that *shinkansen* anime and buys a trans-forming robot toy, only to have it stolen by her young daughter and be forced into a war over who gets it...

Who is this, you ask? My older sister. Even in the real world, there are all sorts of moms.

Early spring 2018, Dachima Inaka

"Mommy swears eternal love!"

Masato's getting married?!
And so is Mamako?!
But who on earth to?!

A cutting-edge momcom adventure!
Next up: the Royal Wedding arc!

Do You Love Your Mom and Her Two-Hit Multi-Target Attacks?

VOLUME 6   Contents subject to change.

ON SALE SUMMER 2020